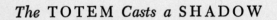

The TOTEM *Casts a* SHADOW

Also by Margaret E. Bell

DANGER ON OLD BALDY

ENEMIES IN ICY STRAIT

THE PIRATES OF ICY STRAIT

WATCH FOR A TALL WHITE SAIL

The TOTEM

Casts a SHADOW

by Margaret E. Bell

Frontispiece by LOUIS DARLING

WILLIAM MORROW AND COMPANY

NEW YORK 1949

This book is for JIM

A U T H O R ' S   N O T E

*T*HE setting of this book is the village of Klink-wan, Alaska, now entirely abandoned. The Indian characters are entirely fictitious. Their names were chosen at random from Haida Indian names appearing on old grave markers. The story is built from a strand of the story of my grandfather's family, who lived in a house similar to the Monroe house in this book. I have tried to present faithfully the Haida Indian village of the 1880's and the relation of the white people of that period to it. I am greatly indebted to Mrs. Helen Sanderson of Hydaburg, Alaska, who made possible my visit to the site of this old village and who assisted me in reconstructing in words the village and my grandfather's house as they must have been in those early days.

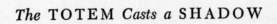

The TOTEM *Casts a* SHADOW

CHAPTER 1

FLORENCE MONROE stood at the upstairs window of the silent house, watching the little steamboat churn her way out through the Narrows. She could see Ma and Laura standing in the stern waving good-by; then Laura's plaidie and the little steamboat itself melted into the thick September fog. Only a blue streamer of smoke was left to show that the *Laura M.* had pulled out for the Mission thirty miles across the tide-ridden bay.

Below the window, Florence could see the two points of land that curved out around the little cove of Klinkwan like the horns of a new moon, leaving a narrow channel through which the tide was flowing steadily in. Beyond the points the islands crowded close on either side of the Narrows and beyond the islands the wide bay was lost in the pearly fog of dawn.

Florence sighed, watching the streamer of smoke thin out as it drifted over the low Indian houses on the north point of the cove. Like the vanishing smoke, her courage was draining away as she realized that she would be alone for the whole day. She stared helplessly at the point where the *Laura M.* had disappeared. Only a little while ago she had hurried up the beach to the house to watch from the upstairs window, as Gregory rowed the skiff out to the steamer. She had seen Pa and Gregory help Ma and Laura up onto the narrow deck of the *Laura M.* and then drag the skiff up across the stern. Now that they were really gone she felt unexpectedly lonely and deserted.

As she stood there alone, her young face was sensitive and grave below the dark auburn curls on her forehead. Her hands rested on the window sill where the diamond on one slender finger caught the light. In a clear, blue spark it seemed to hold all the light of the coming day, and Florence looked down at it, remembering that soon Beldon Craig would be coming back to Klinkwan. With the thought of Beldon came the memory of his fair hair and his blue eyes, the enchantment of his quiet voice, and the knowledge of his love. She forgot the uneasiness that had so suddenly come upon her, and her eyes filled with dreams. The hours would pass quickly and by nightfall the *Laura M.* would come steaming back and Pa would bring the mail from the post office at Howkan. She smiled, thinking of Beldon's letters. They always began, "My dearly Beloved."

Far off to the east the sun was rising over the towering mountains of the Alaskan mainland. Its red-gold light shone over the rugged coast and the dark wooded peaks of Prince of Wales Island. Westward from this island the land gave way to a thousand fog-shrouded islets and finally to the great Pacific Ocean. As the sun rose higher, it colored the fog and burned it off until the mountains of the larger islands rose clear, while the waterways between them still were lost in the golden haze. It was not yet high enough to touch the roof of the Monroe house standing at the head of the little cove of Klinkwan on Prince of Wales Island, or to brighten the fantastic creatures carved on the totem poles of the Indian village.

There was something tender about this island country—tender, and at the same time wild beyond imagining. Its waterways were uncharted; its only town was old Fort Wrangell, a hundred and fifty miles to the north of Klinkwan. In all that island wilderness, the Monroes were the only white family. Their big house, with the lace curtains at its many windows, stood with its back to the forest and the dark mountains. Its long windows looked hopefully southward, ignoring the hostile wilderness and the fierce and laughing faces on the Indian totem poles. It was a dignified house but conspicuous in its white paint, standing, as it did, such a short distance from the low cedar dwellings of the Haida village.

When Ian Monroe had built this house two years ago, in 1886, he believed that other white families would settle in this spot. Its beauty was beyond compare. The red salmon ran upstream to its lakes from the sea in hordes. Its forests were full of fur-bearing animals, and all the riches of the sea were there for the taking. So sure was he that more would come to settle this new country that, in the spring of 1887, he sent for his wife and younger children to leave their comfortable home in Victoria and be the first to establish themselves in this island country. Other Christian families would follow, people who would be an example of right living to the heathen Indians. So far the Indians in Alaska had had little chance to know respectable white people. They had known unscrupulous traders and renegades. Worst of all, they had known squaw men, white men living with Indian women, traitors, Pa said, to all standards of decency.

But now, in the fall of 1888, the Monroes were still the only white family in this island country and Gregory, one of Florence's brothers, said bitterly that if they waited until kingdom come they would still be the only white family there. Why would anyone choose to live in this Godforsaken wilderness when civilization was there to the south? But Pa was still hopeful. Everything comes in its proper time, he said, to those who trust in the Lord. This year he had packed four hundred barrels and twelve hundred half-barrels of salmon at his Hunter Bay saltery only two miles away. He had made arrangements with the Steamship Company, and Alec, his oldest son, and Jaimy, Florence's twin, were waiting now at Hunter Bay for the boat that would take the pack south.

Florence smiled because Beldon Craig was coming to Klinkwan to go south with Pa on his annual buying trip. Beldon's saltery at Thorne Bay on the far side of the island had produced almost as much as Pa's saltery. Florence was proud because Beldon had accomplished so much in one year. She stood, clad in the armor of first love, an armor as shining as that of a young knight, as shining and as untested. I shall be mistress of Thorne Bay, she thought, Beldon Craig's wife and the first bride in all the island country. She gazed absently out of the window, smiling.

With the increasing light of morning the mist all around was suffused with color, and through this enchanting veil the great carved totems looming above the sleeping houses lost their sinister aspect. The low cedar houses of the Indians took on a dreamlike quality, as though they were about to disappear as soon as the sun rose over the hill. Sea

gulls, winging in from the west, dropped out of the
mist with coral feet spread to float, resting, on the
dark water of the cove. A huge raven, perched on
the roof of Pa's store, called raucously and was answered from the forest. The store, standing solidly
between the village and the Monroe house, was at
once the meeting place and the dividing line for
Chief Yelthnow's people and the family of Ian
Monroe, according to their agreement.

A movement at the far end of the point, past the
last totem pole, attracted Florence's eyes. Her
brows drew in to a frown as she saw the Indian
girl Nakatla, the granddaughter of Old Yelthnow,
move higher on the rocks as the tide swirled up to
the place where she had been sitting.

Florence had not known she was there. Even
when she had gone down to the beach to say
good-by to the family none of them had noticed
the Indian girl, so quietly did she sit at the far end
of the curving point. Or had Gregory seen her and
made no sign of it? Florence knew why she was
there, and she tried to shake off the uneasy feeling
the sight of the girl gave her. She knew that in the
evening Nakatla, like herself, would be watching
hopefully for the *Laura M.* to return from the Mission. She would wait all day for a glimpse of Gregory. It was she who had taught him to speak the
Haida language, coming each day to the store with
that excuse for staying there; and Greg, who had
grown withdrawn and silent at home, spent more

and more time in the store. Florence could not bring herself to speak about this, but she thought it strange that Ma had not noticed.

Nakatla was the daughter of a whaler whose ship had been wrecked in the islands. The Indians had found him on the rocks, the sole survivor of that wreck, and brought him back to their village. But when Nakatla's Indian mother died, his discontent grew and he took the first trading ship to come that way, and went to Victoria, taking his baby girl with him. The Indians, unwilling to give up this grand-daughter of a great chief, followed in their huge war canoes and finally, after many months, were able to kidnap the baby and bring her back to her people.

Now Nakatla was seventeen, Florence's own age, yet the girls had spoken to each other only once. Yelthnow's people stayed on their side of the store and the Monroes on the other. Both Yelthnow and Pa were content with this noninterference plan, and the south point of the cove had come to be called Our Point by the Monroe family. But the store was common ground and one day Florence had met Nakatla there.

Gregory had introduced them with the same grace she remembered as his when they lived in Victoria, only there had been irony in his gray eyes and amusement in his voice. She had murmured a greeting, but the Indian girl, overcome with shy-ness, had fled silently on her bare feet out through

the open door and along the plank walk to the village. Florence had had time to see that her eyes
were as gray as Gregory's own, and her legs were
long—not like the island people's.

Uneasily, she watched the girl walk slowly back
along the beach to the great community house of
Chief Yelthnow. It was an old house, low and massive, built with huge cedar timbers and hand-split
boards. In front of the weathered triangular face of
the house there were three totem poles standing in
a row, three sixty-foot cedar trunks carved with the
crests and the animals and birds that represented
the important events in the history of the great
Yelthnow clan. On the top of the middle pole a
gigantic grinning wolf embraced three little men in
its forepaws. This was the traditional totem of the
Yelthnows. The chief and all of his nephews belonged to the wolf clan. Below the wolf a great
killer whale was carved, the symbol of the wife of
Chief Yelthnow. All her sons belonged to the clan
of the killer whales.

Nakatla looked small and wistful standing under
the huge totems, looking across the little cove at the
white Monroe house. Florence drew back from the
window and let the curtain fall over the pane. It
was all very well, she thought resentfully, for Gregory to learn to speak the Indians' language and to
teach them to work in the saltery and to build
houses. But Pa should see that he was doing it because he hated the wilderness and the isolation. Pa

should see that Gregory turned to the Indians because he needed more in his life than working with
his hands.

The big house, with its many rooms, seemed
haunted with silence, and she shivered as she turned
from the window to take off her long blue cloak.
What had happened to this day that she had looked
forward to so short a time before? She had assured
Ma that she would like a day alone, that she would
not be frightened in the least. But now her courage
seemed to have melted away into the fog with the
Laura M. and she was lonely with the uneasy loneliness that comes from being near strange people
whose ways one does not understand. She knew
that Alec and Jaimy were at Hunter Bay and that
she could row there in an hour, but she knew it was
her duty to stay at home. Pa never left the house
unless one of them was there.

Florence had no fear of the wilderness. She loved
the forest and the beach and the rocky islands. She
was nervous because she had never got used to the
Indians. She remembered the stories of their war-
like past, of their heathen ceremonies, and of the
fights that resulted when renegade white men sold
spirits to them. But most of all she was afraid because they knew nothing of God or of Christian
love, and even though Pa was teaching the young
ones to sing the hymns "by the sounds," there was
no way to communicate with them and their ways
were different. There was nothing in the wilderness

so frightening as humankind, no bear or predatory
wolf that chilled one so with legendary fear. She
had got used only to old Mary, who came to help
Ma. She was a slave woman from the Yelthnow
house, who was supposed to come and help with
the heavy work. Sometimes she came early and
started the fires and sometimes she came late.
There were days of feasts or ceremonies in the village when she failed to come at all. But that was
the way of the Indians, and the Monroes had got
used to it. Florence listened now, hoping the old
woman would come.

But instead of the familiar rattle at the kitchen
door, she thought she heard the sound of weird distant chanting. She ran across the hall to Ma's room
where there was a side window looking toward the
innermost end of the village, but she could see only
the store and the sleeping houses. She drew back
the curtain at the front window and looked out
at the shifting fog. People were coming out of the
village now and the dogs were howling. Her own
water spaniel, Donny, was barking and running up
and down the beach below the window.

The chanting grew louder and she saw, coming
in under the golden haze, four great high-prowed
war canoes. Swiftly they came, each driven
through the water by fourteen powerful paddlers.
At the Narrows the leader shot ahead with increased stroke and the others followed in single
file into the entrance to the cove. A shout rose from

the people of the village. They were coming out of all the houses now and running down to the water's edge. Many were half clad and some of the children wore no clothes at all. The old chief and his tiny wife came out of the great community house, wearing ceremonial blankets and tall woven hats, and from the house farthest out on the point came the wizened old medicine man, Quee-aunce. His body was covered with tattoos and streaks of paint.

Then the people stood aside and from the door of the Yelthnow house came Paul, the youngest nephew of the chief, dressed in a dark serge suit and a bowler hat Gregory had given him. He looked more outlandish than all the rest. He walked with his wife, who wore a blanket upon which the design of a bear was outlined with tiny pearl buttons, thousands of tiny pearl buttons bought from the store. They walked down to the edge of the water and stood waiting.

Florence remained at the window, holding the curtain with one hand, pressing the other against her pounding heart. Wide-eyed, she stared at the paddlers in the canoes, at the strange designs tattooed on their bodies and painted on their faces. She stared at the immense eyes and dorsal fins of the killer whale carved on the high, magnificent prows of the canoes. On the beach Donny barked loudly as they came, in stately order, into the little cove.

"Donny!" Florence said. "Stop that! They'll hear

you!" She dropped the curtain and, picking up her skirts, she ran into the hall and down the stairs to call Donny before he attracted attention to the house. At the front door she stopped with her hand on the latch and stood there trembling. She opened the door a crack and called the dog. But Donny was defending the Monroe side of the cove and he was deaf to so faint a call. Laura's little gum boots stood in the hall and Florence picked up one of them and hurled it in his direction. Instantly, he turned and came with his tail waving. "Hush, Donny, hush," she admonished him. As soon as he was inside, she closed the door and shoved in place the unaccustomed bolt. "We've got to stay in and not attract attention," she told him. They won't come on our side of the store, she reassured herself.

She ran through the sitting room and the dining room, carefully drawing the blinds. Then she bolted the kitchen door and with the Monroe cat, McDuff, in her arms and Donny at her heels, she retreated upstairs to the comfort of Ma's room.

The chanting stopped suddenly and the people in the canoes were quiet. On the beach Young Paul stepped forward and began to address them. He talked loud and long, and all eyes were on the suit of clothes he wore.

Florence gazed out through the wide mesh of the lace curtain and slowly she realized what was happening. Gregory had helped Paul lay the foundation of his new house, a cabin built like their own

at Hunter Bay. One night at supper Gregory had
told them that Young Paul was an example of the
new and the old in the Indian village. He would
invite his wife's relations to help him finish the
house and he would pay them with blankets because now he was rich; he had worked for the
Monroes for two years and saved his money. Greg
had said that the other nephews in Yelthnow's house
would not like this because Paul was the youngest,
and setting up a house of his own would give him
importance beyond his years. But Pa approved of
Paul's doing this because he thought it a sign of
progress for the young families to leave the community house and live in houses of their own.
Young Paul was very smart. He would have a mod-
ern house and he would have a totem pole in front
of it, combining the new with the old. He would
have great importance because he was giving this
house-building potlatch.

Nervously, Florence watched as Young Paul
talked. The Indians, including the children, were
utterly silent as they listened. She picked up Pa's
binoculars from their place on the table and looked
at the visitors in their big canoes. The women wore
their blankets wrapped tightly around them but
many of the men were half-naked and most of them
had many tattoos on their bodies and strange bars of
paint on their faces. They must be from the islands
to the south where they had had little of the white
man's influence. Oh, they're a wild-looking lot, she

thought, as she turned the glasses on the group of
old men standing in the stern of the leading canoe.
They were tattooed and painted and on their heads
were woven hats with high cylindrical crowns, but
they wore not one stitch of clothing. With a
shocked little cry, Florence put the binoculars on
the table and drew back from the window.

Uneasily, she paced the floor between the two
windows. She could slip out of the back door and
take the trail across Our Point without being seen.
The little dugout that she and Laura played in was
there, and she could launch it and paddle to Hunter
Bay. Jaimy and Alec were at Hunter Bay. She
could go there and stay at the saltery until evening
or she could make Jaimy come back with her. She
thought of this but she knew she would not do it.
Pa would be displeased if she showed her fear to
the Indians, and besides, her own pride held her
back because she had told them all that she would
not be afraid, that she would enjoy a day to herself.

Young Paul's long speech of greeting was finally
ended and the visitors disembarked. The young
men carried the big canoes high above the tide line
into the long grass and covered them with blankets,
and the women and old men went into the great
community house of Yelthnow.

The mist was almost gone now and the sun was
coming through. Florence looked again toward the
Narrows as though hoping to see the *Laura M.* But
instead of the *Laura M.*, she saw a dugout ap-

proaching the cove, a small dugout paddled by a white man and an Indian woman. She stared, aghast. This must be a—she skipped quickly over the dreadful word—this must be a squaw man. This must be one of the men whom Pa denounced so fiercely. He said they stood for corruption and degradation and that they deserved no respect either from white man or Indian. Let such a one show up at Klinkwan, he said, and he'd drive him off the beach. She remembered then that it was such men as this who sold spirits to the Indians and caused trouble in the villages. Should she go now for Alec? Alec was no hand with the Indians. It was always Gregory or Pa who had dealings with them. Alec would only make things worse if he knew about the squaw man. She decided to wait until evening. She would wait and watch until Pa came home.

C H A P T E R   2

PAUL led the young men to the place where the foundation of his new house was laid. They stood around it while he talked and pointed to the pile of milled lumber beside it. He pointed to the store and to the Monroe house. While he was talking Florence saw the white man. Even from the upstairs window she could not see his dugout but she guessed that it lay beyond the brush on the far side of the point. He came out of the brush, looked around, and then approached the young Indians and spoke to them, pointing in the direction from which he had come. He slapped Young Paul on the back and laughed, and the young Indian laughed and looked toward the Monroe house. Brush grew around the clearing for the new house, protecting it from sight on all sides except the side facing the store. Florence thought the young men looked guilty and self-conscious as they followed the white man into the brush on the far side. She wished Pa were home. Pa would order that man off the beach so fast he wouldn't know what had happened to him. If he had brought drink to sell to the Indians, he would have to be careful because Old Yelthnow was against it, too, and Young Paul knew that. Young Paul had better be careful!

There was nothing to be gained by pacing the floor. Florence looked out through the Narrows again. The mist had burned off and the wide bay sparkled in the sun. The *Laura M.* would be almost to Howkan by now. They were having a fine day for crossing and soon they would be home again. Pa would want her to behave with the dignity and courage befitting a Monroe. In the morning sunlight it was not difficult for her to resolve to stick it out alone until Pa came home.

To keep busy, she started methodically through the upstairs rooms, putting everything in order, meticulously dusting each object, trying not to think. But all the time she was listening, and with each suspended hour, her nerves grew more taut. What are the Indians doing now? she kept asking herself. What are they going to do? She would stop, dustcloth in hand, straining all her senses in

her effort to imagine what was going on in the dark
houses on the point.

In Jaimy's room she dusted each piece of gold ore
and lined them up according to size on the bureau.
In Alec's room she straightened the engraving of
the business section of Victoria, looking absently at
its carriages and its stiff little men in Prince Alberts.
For a moment she felt cheered, remembering that
Alec and Jaimy were at Hunter Bay, but she knew
she wouldn't row to the saltery to tell them she was
frightened. Pa would give her a good lecture if he
thought she had shown fear before the Indians. She
resolved never to let the family know how frightened she was. With this resolution her courage returned, and she felt old and responsible and not
very happy. Like an animal in its lair, fear dwelt
under her courage and she was uneasy and lonelier
than she had ever thought she could be. She went
on to Gregory's room, fortified with a determination
akin to Pa's own.

Greg's room was full of things he called Indian
art, things that the rest of the family called curios.
He had made himself a big table, and over this,
hanging on the wall, was a huge woven Indian hat.
On either side of it were rattles carved in the shape
of ravens with great heads and beaks and small
wings folded back over their bodies no larger than
Florence's fist. Below them on the table there was
a bottle of ink and a pen and some music script with
notes and Haida words written under them. Above

the bed two grotesque wooden masks grinned down and Florence wondered how her brother could bear to sleep beneath them. On the bureau, in an oval frame, was a picture of Frances Whitehall. She had given it to Gregory the year he left Victoria. It had been months—almost a year now—since Frances had written Gregory. Florence knew that he would never ask her to live in this wild country, although the Monroe fortune was in Alaska now. Greg said nothing but he had grown taciturn and bitter, hating the isolation and the wilderness. This picture and the music sheets were the only defenses against the strong and fierce design of the Indian things already dominating his room.

Sudden shouting and the abrupt sound of hammering startled Florence out of her memories. In Gregory's room one window faced the store and the inmost end of the Indian village. From this window she saw that the Indian men had gathered around the foundation of the new house and many women stood watching them as Young Paul instructed them in building the framework. Paul had helped Greg build the cabin at the Hunter Bay saltery, and now he strode about full of pride, showing off his newly acquired knowledge. Soon the tattooed bodies of his friends were shining with sweat, and the framework began to rise amid much noise and yelling and the admiration of the watchers. Florence had heard these potlatches described as wild heathen orgies which often got out of control, especially if the In-

dians had spirits to drink. Greg had said that they
were not heathen orgies but formal ceremonies carried on in connection with building the house and
raising the totem pole. It took great wealth to give
a potlatch. This was the first one to be given at
Klinkwan since the Monroes had come there to live.
Florence had heard that the celebrating went on
for days.

Finding courage in the knowledge that Pa and
the family would be home by nightfall, Florence
sat all afternoon on the edge of the rocker in Ma's
room and hemstitched, while the Indians hammered
away on Paul's new house. She sat tense and rigid
and her work lagged because she paused often to
listen and to look out of the windows. All afternoon
she waited, solitary in this land and alien to its people, like the Monroe house itself.

Early in the evening she went to the kitchen and
made preparations for the family supper, because
the darkness would come early to the rear rooms
and she intended to light no lamps until the family
were home again. They would be in sometime during the long twilight between the setting of the sun
and the dark. She began to feel hopeful now because, so far, all had gone well and soon, oh, very
soon, they would be home. Impatiently, she waited
for the sun to go down. When the kitchen was in
order, she set the drafts on the stove and then flew
upstairs to look out through the Narrows. But the
rays of the sun, deep now in the west, were blinding

and she turned her eyes toward the Indian houses where smoke poured out of the roof vents and drifted lazily over the cove. The tide had run low in the cove and there was only thirty feet of water between the rocky points. Inside the points the black shale beach sloped steeply down to water as still and dark as a pond.

The hammering on Young Paul's house stopped and the Indians stood for a moment talking together. Then, casting many looks in the direction of Yelthnow's house, they went quickly and stealthily to the far side of the point and disappeared in the brush. Florence watched apprehensively, fearing that even Old Yelthnow would not be able to control the young Indians if they actually were buying alcohol from the squaw man. The shadows on the ground deepened and the red rays of the sinking sun slanted briefly across the tops of the totem poles, casting a lurid glow on the grinning face of the great wolf. Its long fangs turned red for a moment and then, in the afterglow, only the enormous eyes glistened.

The sun had gone down. Anxiously, Florence looked out toward the bay, praying for a sight of the *Laura M.* The thin clouds in the west turned into streamers of red and gold. The water in the Narrows and in the cove seemed lacquered in flame, and farther out the bay was alight with color. The mountains of the distant islands were black against the light and, gradually, the reflected color on the water withdrew until it lingered only on the open places. The totems before the houses of the village grew dark and shadowed with mystery, and from the community house of Yelthnow came the beat of drums and the wild, eerie chant of the Indians. People began coming out of the other houses, the people of Klinkwan and their guests. In blankets and headdress they came and, two by two, entered the low door of the big house. Boldly, Florence pulled back the curtain. Any minute now she would see the *Laura M.* She waited, and still the little steamer did not come but, black against the glowing surface of the water, she recognized the departing dugout paddled by the white man and the Indian woman. Oh, Lord, she prayed, bring the family home soon.

The golden light had faded and beneath the clouds the sky made a pale clear band. There, in the west, the new moon floated like a delicate, mystic boat. Florence thought again of Beldon and the letters Pa would bring. She looked down at her ring, trying not to think of the worry that began to assail her. The room grew darker and the beat of the drums picked up and took on a singular rhythm. When she looked up again, the night had gathered in the dome of the sky and a few faint stars trembled there. The little moon was sailing down behind the far-off mountains and the rim of light grew dim. Soon it would be dark, too dark for the *Laura M.* to come in through the Narrows.

As Florence watched the night rise like black

haze out of the forests and the pale green band of light remaining in the south sink into the ocean, the fear that had lurked within her all day began to bring every frightening possibility to mind. Suppose the *Laura M.* had broken down; suppose the boiler had burst and scalded them all. Suppose the tide had carried them into the rocks. Something dreadful must have happened. They would not leave her alone at night—even Pa would not expect her to stay alone at night.

Her fear painted every possible disaster until her heart was pounding and her desolation too great to bear. She resolved to go to Hunter Bay and tell the boys. She would take the trail to the other side of Our Point, where her own little dugout was kept, and launch it and paddle to the saltery. She would wait just a little longer to be sure.

The tide was filling the cove again and the inexorable darkness deepening when, with a shout, a fire was lit on the beach in front of the Indian houses. Its flames leapt up, lighting the fantastic faces on the totem poles so that, in the flickering light, the great white-rimmed eyes and the huge teeth seemed to blink and grin as the half-naked Indians ran in and out of the glow, shouting and wrestling with one another. Florence stared, wide-eyed, so frightened now that she dared not leave the house.

Behind her in the dark room Donny whined, and she turned and sank down on the floor beside him.

He thrust his cold, wet nose into her hands, and she put both arms around him and wept against his smooth, sympathetic head. Then, faintly, she heard a knock on the kitchen door and she held her breath, listening.

The knock came again, unmistakable and persistent, and Florence got to her feet. She stood with her hands clasped tightly together, staring into the dark hall. "I'll have to go down," she whispered. "Pa would hate me to be afraid." The knock came once more, this time more insistent. "I'll have to go down," she said again, almost without feeling. She struck a match and lit the lamp. When she replaced the chimney and adjusted the wick, the familiar objects in the room seemed to jump into being and establish her world again, the world of the Monroe house.

With a sharp intake of breath she cried, "Donny, to heel, sir!" and she marched into the hall and down the stairs, holding the lamp above her head. She walked swiftly and resolutely lest her fear overtake her. She went through the dining room and across the kitchen with a firm step, but at the door her courage failed and her hand trembled on the latch.

"Who is it?" she asked, before she could stop herself.

The reply came in soft, hesitating English. "It is—only—Nakatla—please."

Florence's relief was akin to joy. Quickly, she

opened the door and the light of her lamp fell on the face of the Indian girl. Florence stepped back into the room and they looked at each other shyly. "Won't you come in?" she asked.

Nakatla remained on the threshold. She was so overcome with shyness that she seemed unable to speak and stood looking down at her bare feet and squeezing her small brown hands together. Her full purple skirt came to her ankles and she wore a pink waist that hung loosely over it. Her gold earrings were carved in the wolf design and many strings of blue beads hung around her neck. Nakatla looked alarmed every time the shouting on the beach reached a crescendo.

"Yelthnow not like," she said, suddenly looking up. "Come. The ladies in Yelthnow house make place for you. Yelthnow's wife say come."

Completely unprepared for this invitation, Florence had no idea what Nakatla meant. She was appalled at the thought of going to the Indian house. To go alone—with all those painted savages? Why, it was unthinkable. Nervously, she put the lamp on the table. "Please come in," she said, turning to Nakatla. She tried with all her might to be composed.

The granddaughter of Old Yelthnow stepped hesitantly into the room and little spots of light flashed from the many bracelets on her arms and from the beads around her neck. Her dark gray eyes were frightened and sad as she looked at Flor-

ence and looked away again, blushing with embarrassment.

Then she began to talk rapidly and urgently.
"Mr. Monroe not come. Too late now. No mother
—no sister. Not good to be alone. Yelthnow's wife
say you come. She keep you safe."

Florence was conscious of the omission of Gregory's name, and there was something sinister in the
"No mother—no sister." "What has happened?" she
asked. "Do you know what has become of the
Laura M. ?"

Nakatla seemed frightened by these questions
and drew back, saying nothing.

"Please," Florence coaxed, "tell me."

"They come tomorrow, maybe," Nakatla said.
"The ladies make place in big house for you. You
safe there."

Florence knew that there was an element of
safety in being with the Haida women. They had
authority and dignity in their clans. But she was
loath to leave the house. It seemed like deserting
and it made her feel ashamed. The decision was
made for her as a fresh burst of yelling and the fir-
ing of shots came from the beach.

With her eyes on the floor, Nakatla said,
"Stranger bring whiskey."

"I'll get my cape," Florence said, knowing that
indeed it would not be safe to stay alone in the
house. She had waited too long to try to get to

Hunter Bay. The whole situation had got out of hand and she knew it was filled with danger. Moving as though propelled by some force quite outside herself, she got her cape and returned to the kitchen.

C H A P T E R   3

*I*N THE sudden darkness after the lamp was out Florence fought down her impulse to run and hide. It was too late now to do anything but pray; and pray she did as she closed the door, leaving Donny behind her. Outside, the forest shadowed the walk, making the night seem darker than it was. The yells of the Indians filled the air, and lurid firelight kept leaping across the boardwalk between the Monroe house and the store as the flames of the beach fire rose and fell. Nakatla led the way swiftly along the walk past the store and Florence followed uncertainly, holding her long dark cape around her. For the first time she found herself going beyond

Pa's store into the territory of Old Yelthnow. A
little way beyond the store the walk left off suddenly and the Indian trail began.

The sound of the drums and the chanting grew
louder and wilder and Florence wrapped her cloak
more tightly around her. Like someone hypnotized
or in a trance, she followed the Indian girl along the
trail back of the houses. As they drew close to the
great bulk of Old Yelthnow's house Florence tried
to gather her routed thoughts into some kind of
order. I'll try to behave like Ma, she told herself;
I'll get through it somehow—God will help me.

As they turned in to the low door in the corner
of the house she tried to remember the things that
Gregory had told her about the Indians: that they
were a people of formal manners, proud and easily
offended; that their stony faces were only for the
whites or for their enemies. Greg said they had
capacity for deep emotion and could not be controlled if they were really stirred up. But the Monroes were not their enemies, she told herself. Pa
was Old Yelthnow's friend.

Nakatla opened the low door and Florence, bending her head, followed her into the house. The
singular rhythm of the drums filled the murky in-
terior and set her heart to fluttering with a fearful,
curious excitement. Smoke assailed her nostrils and
with it the smell of dried fish, seaweed, eulochon
oil, and the animal smell of many bodies. With an
involuntary gesture she covered her nose with her

white linen handkerchief; then, hastily, she took it
down lest someone see and be offended. She stood
on the top floor of the house, a sort of gallery built
all the way around the timber walls and extending
out for fifteen feet. There it dropped off to another
level about three feet below. The second level was
not so wide and it reached around the rectangular
earthen floor at the bottom of the excavation. On
the ground two fires burned and Indian women
worked near them. Between the back wall of the
house and the edge of the top floor level there hung
a wide mat and a pattern board on which were
painted the conventional Indian designs. Drums
throbbed and the shuffling of feet could be heard.
Otherwise the house was silent and the wild cries
outside seemed far away and unimportant. The
drummers were hidden from Florence's view by the
hanging mat, but by looking past it she could see
the great carved tree trunks that supported the massive roof. The wolf symbol appeared on each one
of them and sometimes there were other figures.

People sat around the upper level in the gloom,
watching the lighted place in front of the mat where
the drummers sat, and the drums throbbed and beat
softly until the house seemed alive and this lighted
place its heart. Florence could see the painted
faces of the chieftains and their wives, who sat in
places of honor. Nakatla had gone off silently on
her bare feet and Florence was alone. She stifled a

sudden impulse to bolt out of the door and fly for home.

A massive totem stood on either side of the mat in front of her and in the corner opposite the place where she had come in new blankets were hung over a frame, making a cubicle like the sleeping compartments of the Indians. In the light that slanted between the totem and the blankets, Florence saw Nakatla returning with the wife of Chief Yelthnow. The tiny old woman wore a long skirt and over it hung a bright silk waist such as Pa sold in his store. She glittered with silver and gold beads. She passed between the great carved storage chests, stopping in front of Florence, and began to talk, standing erect with her hands clasped lightly together. She talked for some time in the Haida language.

When she finished Nakatla said, "She tell you not be afraid—you safe in this house like her daughter."

Florence murmured, "Thank you," but she was at a loss for words, feeling that more than this was expected of her. "Please tell her I am grateful," she added. "I don't know what has happened to my family, but when—if—my father comes back he will thank her." She felt inadequate and stumbling and she could feel the color creeping into her cheeks.

Nakatla translated the words to her grandmother but she seemed to be saying much more. When the old woman replied it was at length, and Florence stood all this while, remembering that she must up-

hold the dignity of the Monroe house. When the
old woman finished, Nakatla smiled, showing fine
white teeth. "She say they come—maybe tomorrow.
You safe with Haida ladies."

They led her across the house behind the hanging
mat to the cubicle made with the blankets. The
chief's wife drew back one of the blankets and
Florence saw that it was new and fine like the
blankets they themselves had brought from Victoria. Inside the cubicle there was a bed made with
new white sheets turned back over the blankets and
there was a pillow with a white linen slip. Beside
the bed a little coal-oil lamp burned cheerfully on
a low stool.

The chief's wife spoke again and Nakatla translated. "She say you eat—I bring food—then sleep."

Yelthnow's wife watched Florence's face intently
as the girl translated and Florence tried to show her
appreciation. She bowed to the little old lady and
said to the girl, "Please tell her I thank her. It is
very nice—just like home."

Nakatla took some time to translate this and the
chief's wife smiled with pleasure and departed,
dropping the blanket curtain and leaving Florence
alone in the cubicle, with the little lamp glowing on
the low stool beside her.

She stood there thinking of nothing at all, feeling
too strange for any emotion save bewilderment.
She stared at the blanket the chief's wife had let
drop across the entrance to her little room. Then

the curtain was drawn aside again and she started
back in fright. But it was only old Mary, the slave
woman—old Mary who came sometimes to help Ma.

The sight of the old servant seemed to Florence
like an answer to her prayer. "Oh, Mary," she whispered, "I'm so glad to see you!"

The old woman carried a tray upon which re-
posed a bone china teapot and a cup. Beside them
on a plate lay two long strips of smoked salmon.
Old Mary giggled as she put the tray on the end of
the narrow bed. "Fix like in Monroe house," she
said. This seemed to amuse her and her giggles
broke into laughter. Mary had learned some English and a great deal about the way the Monroe
house was run. "Indian supper," she said and departed, still laughing.

Florence supposed it was funny, but it wasn't
funny enough to make her laugh. Nevertheless she
was sorry old Mary had gone and she was less fearful because she had been there. She sat on the edge
of the bed and poured tea into the cup and after
drinking it she felt brave enough to be curious.

She stood up and cautiously drew the blanket
aside, just a crack, and looked out. She found that
she was looking right across in front of the two giant
totems that supported the roof at the rear of the
house. One of them was so close to her that she
could see the adz marks on the wood. The mat behind which she had entered the house hung between the carved posts and in front of it three girls

were dancing. But it wasn't the dancers or the drummers behind them or the leaping shadows on the mat that held Florence's fascinated eyes. She gazed at the two lamps that stood there, one at the base of each carved post. Calmly they glowed, like Christian altarpieces, casting their light upward on the great beaks and toothy snouts on the totems. They were lamps from Pa's store with clear, slender chimneys projecting upward through the spherical shades with roses painted upon them. They looked fragile and symbolic under the huge heraldic emblems of the Yelthnow house and Florence remembered what the Reverend Douglas, the missionary at Howkan, had said: "It is for us to bring the Light to the heathen darkness."

Slowly she let the curtain drop and sank back upon the narrow bed. The smoke in the air was stinging her nose and her eyes. She smoothed her handkerchief on her lap to try to make it fresh again. Outside in the big room the drums stopped abruptly and there were shouts and cries and then all was silent. A man's voice began talking. It was a young voice, full of bravado, and through the smooth flow of Haida words she heard Pa's name spoken several times. When the speech ended, the room was filled with excited murmurs and conversation. Then to her unbelieving ears came the tune of one of Pa's favorite hymns.

She got up, feeling weak-kneed and weary, and peeked through the crack in her curtain. There

between the great staring totems stood Pa's choir.
They all wore civilized clothing, as Pa demanded of
them when they came to the store to practice on
Sunday morning, and they stood as he had taught
them in order to sing their parts. In front, Young
Paul stood conducting them. He swayed tipsily but
his face was earnest and proud. The voices of the
singers were true and beautiful and they sang in
harmony without accompaniment; but try as she did
Florence could not make out the words, sung as
they were in a combination of Scottish and Haida
accents. The tattooed audience sat listening intently; even the young men who had come in with
Paul were quiet, leaning against the wall, listening.

Florence couldn't understand the words but she
didn't need to. She knew them by heart. She
dropped the curtain and sank back on the bed, feeling suddenly more lonely and deserted than ever,
as the familiar words ran through her mind.

> *Blest be the tie that binds*
> *Our hearts in Jesus' love.*

How true their voices were! And how impossible
that they should be singing a hymn in this great
murky room with the totems looming above them
and the feast being prepared on the earth floor below them.

Hysterical after the long, harrowing day, Florence began to laugh. But her laughter soon turned
to tears and she sat on the narrow bed weeping

silently into her hands. When the hymn ended and
the excited shouts proclaimed it the best thing of
the evening, she paid no heed but wept on, quite
unable to control the loneliness that filled her heart.

The feasting and yelling went on all night and,
too weary to weep more, Florence looked longingly
at the white sheets. But she could not bring herself
to undress. Enveloped in her several layers of
clothing, she felt that she at least had her dignity;
that if anyone came to look in she would be protected by this sign of her station. Finally she blew
out the little lamp, lay down on top of the blankets,
and drew her cape over her tired body. She resolved to rest and to wait and when all was quiet
to return to her own home.

It was nearly morning before the celebrating and
feasting ended and the guests went away to the
various houses where they were to sleep. Only the
chiefs and the aristocrats and their families
remained in the house of Yelthnow. They slept according to their station: the chiefs in little compartments like Florence's and the others on the floor of
the second level of the big community house. The
servants and those who had been slaves slept in the
front near the door, the lowest station of all. When
the house finally quieted down, the gray light of
dawn was showing through the smoke hole and outside the ravens could be heard giving their morning
call, repeating and answering with articulate voices.

CHAPTER 4

*T*HERE was no early rising in the village of
Klinkwan after such a feast. Many ceremonies were
yet to come, the tattooing of the children, the raising of the totem pole, and, last but most important,
the distribution of blankets to those who had
worked on the new house. Young Paul had bought
many blankets at Pa's store. The giving away of
blankets for the building of the house would make
him a house chief, which was a great advance for
the youngest nephew of the chief. But this morning
Young Paul slept heavily after rendering the night
loud with song and shouting.

Florence had fought sleep as long as she could.

She had lain waiting for the morning and while she
was waiting had fallen into a sleep of utter ex-
haustion. But soon she was awakened by excited
shouting and a great hubbub in the house. She
woke, startled and uncomprehending, sniffing the
unfamiliar air. Light streamed down through the
smoke hole, but little of it reached the deep corners
of the house and in the dark protection of her
blanket walls Florence thought it was still night.
She got up stiffly, remembering slowly all that had
happened during that endless night. Her bones
ached and her eyes were so heavy they kept closing,
and she had to make an effort to keep them open.
She peeked timidly through the crack between the
blankets and saw to her amazement the bright day-
light streaming down through the smoke hole.
Some of the people were crowding out through the
low door at the front of the house and the women
on the different floor levels were calling to each
other. Florence drew back, puzzled and uneasy,
wondering why Nakatla had not come to wake her.
Nervously, she tried to get her hair in order and to
smooth the wrinkles out of her clothes. She
frowned, trying to gather her forces for a move.

Then she heard a voice at once familiar and
strange. In a moment she recognized the voice; it
was Gregory's but it sounded different because he
was talking in Haida and the strange phonetics of
the language seemed to change the very tone of his
voice. Or was she dreaming? With a flustered little

movement she pulled the blanket aside and looked out. She saw her brother and the Indian girl Nakatla walking toward her on the upper level of the floor. Below them on the lower platform, women were folding blankets and talking to each other in urgent voices with a great sound of chattering. Down on the earth floor others were building the fires, and smoke rose slowly across the light to the wide vent in the roof. Gregory was talking earnestly to the girl and he did not see Florence until she stepped out from her blanket shelter. Then he turned away from Nakatla and hurried toward her, smiling.

She stood in the dim smoky light and looked at him. As he drew near her he became serious, his sensitive face changing as quickly as his thought. "Why, Flossie," he said, "what's the matter? You look as if you'd seen a ghost."

She said, "Oh, Greg, what happened?"

"The Reverend's school in Howkan burned. It was pretty awful. We had to stay and help." He smiled at her encouragingly. "They took care of you, didn't they? I kept telling Ma they would." Behind him Nakatla was watching them with shy, almost frightened eyes.

Florence gazed at her brother as one looks at some familiar object after waking from a nightmare. "Oh, Greg, please take me home," she said in a weak voice.

When Yelthnow's wife came up the short ladder

from the lower level it seemed to Florence that she
was reappearing as out of a dream. She took hold
of Greg's arm for reassurance. "Thank her for me,
Greg," she whispered. "I was frightfully scared, but
she was very kind."

Gregory spoke to the tiny old woman in her own
language. For a while they talked seriously. Then
they laughed and seemed to be joking with each
other, and suddenly Florence felt oddly excluded.
Greg seemed happier here with these people than
he did at home. She looked at him as though she
were seeing him for the first time.

The chief's wife spoke seriously again to Greg
and looked at Florence. Then she summoned
Nakatla, and together they descended the little ladder to the lower level of the floor. Gregory returned
the girl's lingering glance with a smile. "Thank
you, Nakatla," he said in English. "You are a good
girl."

To Florence Greg said, "Come, we'll go the back
way. The old lady has just told me to take you back
to your own clan." He laughed and squeezed her
arm. "Come, silly, don't look so scared."

Outside, the morning light drained down through
folds of high white fog. The cove was brimming
full, and the beach was covered with water right up
to the tall beach grass. The air smelled only of the
forest, of cedar and of moss. Florence breathed
deeply of its sweetness and shook herself, trying to
rid her clothing of the smell of smoke.

Greg looked at her. "I wish I'd had your chance to stay in that house all night—and a potlatch night, too."

"Oh, Greg, don't tease," she said. In the revealing light she could see that he was tired. He was the only man in the Monroe family who was cleanshaven, except Jaimy, of course, who was still downy. He was just a little taller than she, and he turned and looked at her and she saw the amusement fade out of his eyes.

"I'm not teasing," he said. "I've never seen a house-building potlatch—and now they're all paddling away to see the results of the fire at Howkan. Young Paul will be sore as an owl to have his potlatch interrupted."

"Oh, they'll come back," Florence said, "and they'll be howling and yelling all night, and I suppose you'll like that. Oh, Greg, how can you!"

They had passed the half-finished house now and they could see the big canoes leaving the cove. Greg stopped to watch the high-prowed craft, propelled by many eager paddlers, shoot out through the Narrows. "They'll race each other to Howkan," he mused, apparently not heeding his sister's agitation. "I hope Young Paul won't lay this to the white man's bad luck. He's learned a lot from us, you know. But he'll still heed the words of the medicine man."

Florence pulled him on to the boardwalk.

"Please, Greg! Do let's get home. Who cares what he thinks of the medicine man?"

Greg remained silent and Florence felt uneasily that he was a good deal concerned about what Paul thought of the medicine man. His silence made her feel ashamed of being flippant. "I didn't mean that, really," she said, "but Greg, I do worry about you."

They were passing the store now and she hurried because she didn't want to face Pa until she'd got a chance to tidy up. She looked at Greg's handsome profile with its pale golden skin and sooty lashes. His sensitive mouth was becoming set in stubborn, defensive lines and his dark gray eyes looked out from under straight black brows with such searching challenge that even Florence felt uneasy when they were turned upon her.

Greg had never forgiven Pa for bringing them all to Alaska. It had been Greg's dream to go to Edinburgh to study—to live, he had said. But Pa had always been a pioneer. Ever since he left Scotland he had been searching for new worlds. There could be no understanding between Pa and Gregory, with Greg longing to go back to the old and civilized places and Pa turning away from them to seek always the untarnished and the new.

"I wish Pa would let you go away from here," she ventured timidly.

"Don't be a ninny," Greg said. "Where Pa goes the Monroes go. Cheer up, Flossie. He's got a couple of letters for you from Bel. Don't let him see how scared you are. Look, the sun is shining, even on this benighted land."

"Beldon will say when he's coming to go south with Pa on the boat. Oh, Greg, I hope he comes soon." She gave him a sidelong glance, thinking of Beldon and Thorne Bay and Pa's new world. "And besides," she added, "this isn't a benighted land—if you stay in your proper place."

"Oh, yes, it *is* a benighted land. There wouldn't be any proper place if it weren't. Oh, I know Pa's rule. We stay on one side and the Indians on the other. But just keep it up long enough and we'll end by hating each other." Greg jumped off the walk and started off through the tall beach grass growing between the store and the Monroe house. "Run along home and shake the heathen smoke out of your hair. Tell Ma I've gone to get Jaimy to help take the grub to Howkan."

Florence picked up her skirts and ran along the walk. She would try to talk to Ma about Greg. This would be a good time to tell her that something should be done about Greg. The kitchen door was open. Pale and wide-eyed, Florence flew into Ma's arms.

"Praise be!" cried Ma, hugging her tall daughter. "My, I'm glad to see you home. Gracious, child, you smell like a smoked salmon!"

They both began to laugh, clinging to each other and rocking back and forth while Donny ran around them in circles, barking for attention. On

the big range the teakettle sang merrily, and light
streamed through the windows upon the white ship-
lap walls. On a damask cloth the thin china was
laid out invitingly, the pink roses on the teacups
signifying the ways of a more conventional world.

There was a rush at the dining-room door and
little Laura came running into the kitchen. Her
bright gold curls were held back by a blue ribbon
and her round green eyes took in the scene with
the expanding awareness of the eleven-year-old.
Within the door she stopped and laughed.

"Donny's got his paws on your bustle, Sister," she
giggled. "You *do* look funny."

Florence lifted her cheek from Ma's neat head
and turned to calm Donny. "Do stop giggling,
Laura, and run up and get the water jug from our
room, there's a good girl." She slipped her cape off.
"I'll hang this on the line to air now."

"Were you all night in the Indian house?" Laura
asked breathlessly. "Really, were you?"

Ma said, "Run along now and get the jug. Florence will tell us all about it when she's freshened."

With a flick of her curls Laura was off upstairs.
Florence threw her cape over the line in the garden
and returned. "Oh, I do smell horrid!" she sighed.
"That house was full of smoke and fish."

"I'll pour you a cup of tea," Ma offered. "You're
still overwrought. Goodness, what a night we all
had!"

"Oh, Ma, I was so scared," Florence confided.

"And Old Yelthnow's wife knew it. She sent that girl, Nakatla, over here to get me. She took care of me—you know, as a neighbor would. But it was so strange, I was frightened all the time. And Ma, a white man came in a dugout with an Indian woman. I think—I couldn't see them, you know—but I think they sold spirits to Young Paul."

"Pa will be angry about that," Ma said.

"And Ma," Florence went on, hoping that she would understand, "when Gregory came into Yelthnow's house this morning with that girl, I had the funniest feeling about him. Oh, Ma, Greg has changed! I had the feeling that he'd been so much with the Indians that he, well, that he was growing to be like them. I do wish Pa would send Greg away."

Quickly Ma said, "Men can go about places, dear, and be quite unchanged, really. Gentlemen have roamed the far corners of the earth and been quite unchanged. But it is different with a lady. A lady must have home and protection. Gregory will be all right, dear. It was just that you were overwrought. If anyone goes south I'm afraid it will be Laura. Pa thinks she should go to school."

Laura came in at the end of Ma's little speech and Florence sank wearily down on a chair. It was as she feared; no one would believe that Greg had changed so much. Laura put the big water jug on the table and came and stood in front of her sister. "Were they really as wild as they looked this morn-

ing in those big canoes?" she asked. "Were you
really *frightfully* scared?"

Florence looked at her little sister and found herself wishing Laura to understand that the Indians
had been kind and that they had *meant* to be so.
"They were very nice," she explained. "The chief's
wife made me a bed within an enclosure. It was
just . . . that it was so strange," she ended lamely.

"Florence was very brave," Ma said with cheerful finality. "She was worried about us and she's
tired. Now run out and gather the strawberries for
me."

Obediently, Laura got the basket and started for
the door. "Well," she said, "at least *we* had the fire,
but I think the Indians were better. I suppose it'll
be a blue moon before anything happens around
here again."

Upstairs, in the chill of her own room, Florence
removed her clothing. Then, in her blue wrapper,
she ran across the hall to the cheerful warmth of
Ma's room. Standing with her back to the little iron
stove she could feel the coldness drain away from
her skin. Through the lace curtains the last of the
departing canoes were dimly visible and Greg had
already pulled out for the short run to Hunter Bay.
In the village only the old people and the children
were left.

Florence spread a bath towel on the floor and let
the wrapper slip from her shoulders. She poured
the warm water into the basin. "What a ninny I

am," she whispered to herself. "How could I have been so scared?" She began sponging her face and neck, using the rose-scented soap on Ma's commode. As she splashed the warm water on her face she started to live the day and night over again in a dream in which she behaved with mature composure at every turn of events. But the dream slipped away and she thought of her letters, tucked in one of Pa's pockets, and knew she wouldn't get them until Pa had discussed the whole thing with her because Pa took everything in its "proper order." Leaning forward, she rested her knuckles on the hard warm bottom of the basin and, squeezing the sponge on her shoulder, let the scented, soapy water run smoothly down her arm.

FLORENCE came through the kitchen with her arms full of clothing. "Oh, Ma," she said, "Do you think this dress will ever air out? I'll put the cottons to soak and they'll be all right."

"It'll air out all right," said Ma, "if the weather holds."

Florence put her petticoats and underthings, even her stays, into the tub in the shed at the back of the house. She took her dress to the garden, where she found Laura not picking strawberries, but playing with a pair of toads. "Laura," she exclaimed, "you'll get warts! Put those things down. The boys'll be here any minute and you've not picked a straw-berry."

Laura reluctantly and gently put her toads in among the strawberry vines. "I don't feel like picking," she sighed. "You should have seen the fire! The school and the place where they keep their supplies burned right down to nothing but ashes. It began while we were eating with the Reverend and Mrs. Douglas." She looked up and went on, teasingly. "They talked about you and Beldon."

Florence stopped shaking her dress and looked down at her little sister. "Who talked? What did they say?"

"The Reverend and Pa did most of the talking," Laura confided, "but they hadn't time to really get under way when the fire started and the Indians began to yell."

"What did they *say*?" Florence asked, making an effort to keep her patience.

"Oh, it was about your wedding. You'll know soon enough," Laura teased.

"What an imp you are, Laura! It's high time you were sent out to school!" Pa and the boys were coming along the walk and she hoped Laura would go in because she dreaded the childish scrutiny during her meeting with Pa. "It's too late to pick strawberries now," she said. "Ma will have to open a tin of plums. Do go in and help her."

She made her way through the rows of beet and turnip tops to meet the Monroe men. How alike they were, Alec and Jaimy and Pa, all tall and redheaded, all with red whiskers—you could see that

Jaimy's would be red when they grew. Alec was
more angular than the other two, not having quite
the breadth of shoulder. He was a serious, responsible fellow and he kept his red beard trimmed
Prince Albert style and so did Pa. Jaimy, her twin,
laughed more than any of them and he was laughing now, as he talked to Greg. Only Gregory was
different, slight and graceful and dark like Ma, a
black Scot among the red Monroes.

Pa approached Florence, looking at her critically.
He stood six feet three inches and he had that
authority about him that is found in military officers,
headmasters, and others whose position is undis-
puted. "Flossie," he said, "I'll speak wi' ye a moment."

"Yes, Pa," Florence said, glad that she had
changed and freshened up.

Before anything further could be said Laura
squealed, "Oh, Jaimy! Flossie's going to be married
in the Howkan church, as an example to the Indians!
The Reverend said so."

"Keep peace, child," said Pa. "You're to speak
when you're spoken to and not interrupt your elders. Off to the house now and help your ma."

Laura went into the kitchen, scowling, and Jaimy
burst out laughing. "Wait until Bel hears that one,"
he cried.

Pa stood looking down at Florence with eyes
much like her own, hazel eyes with long straight
lashes that veiled them when cast down. Under his

penetrating gaze she looked down and felt the color
tingling in her face. Pa always made her feel guilty,
as though she had been caught in some cowardly
act. And yet she knew he was fair and considerate,
according to his lights.

"And what's all this," he asked, "aboot going to
the Indian house while we were awa'?"

In the light of day, with the whole family at
home, her experience of the night before seemed so
unreal that she felt confused and could find no justification for her terror. "Oh, Pa," she said, "when it
got dark and you didn't come I thought something
terrible had happened to you and I was scared."
She paused and he was silent. She could tell that
he considered this not nearly justification enough
for leaving home and going to the village. "The
Indians made so much noise . . . and all those
strange ones came . . ."

"Come, child," he interrupted. "You're standing
there like a scairt mousie. Tell me all of it now,
from the start."

So she began at the beginning and told him the
events of the day. When she got to the part where
she saw the white man and the Indian woman come
in through the Narrows and go around to the other
side of the point, Pa stopped her.

"Mind what ye say now!" Pa said sharply. "Ye
saw this squaw man take spirits to the Indians?"

"I saw him talk to them and later they began

shouting and quarreling." She saw Pa's eyes harden with anger.

"It is hard to believe that Yelthnow would permit . . ." Pa stopped as though he thought she was mistaken.

"I don't think he knew it until later," Florence hastened to explain. "It was only Young Paul and some of the strangers and a few of the men of the village. Yelthnow was displeased—I could see him talking to Paul on the beach—and after that they went back to work and didn't begin yelling again until evening, and then the"—she couldn't bring herself to say the revolting word—"the white man left."

"He's no white man," Pa said, and she could see that he was furious even though his voice was not loud. It was hard and implacable, full of anger. "He's a squaw man, and this is what you expect of such. I'll demand that Yelthnow send Paul off the place for patronizing such a r-r-renegade." When Pa was angry his r's rolled even longer than at other times.

"Yelthnow's wife was very kind, Pa," Florence ventured. She told Pa the whole story, even about Young Paul tipsily leading the choir and how well they sang. This seemed to mollify him a little but she could see that he was not pleased with her behavior.

"In the future," he said, "ye'll stay in our ain house, as becomes a Monroe. No matter what goes on in yon village."

He started into the house and Florence followed him, glad that she had escaped a long lecture. "Were—were there any letters for me, Pa?" she asked, hopefully.

"Aye," said Pa. "We must not wait now. After the meal ye may have them."

The flurry of putting the food on the table was soon over and the Monroe family stood around the table back of their chairs. Pa waited until all the rustling had stopped and then he asked God to bless their food and to make them useful in His service, Amen. Pa pushed his chair behind him and picked up the carving knife and all the rest of them sat down, Ma behind the huge silver tea service, Jaimy and Florence at her right, and Laura, Gregory, and Alec opposite them. With the exception of Ma's, all eyes were on the big venison roast as Pa carved. When the tea was poured, Ma sent the cups along from her end of the table while the plates came up from Pa's end. As the plates passed, Florence heaped them with potatoes and rutabagas from their own garden. Hot biscuits and wild currant jelly passed from hand to hand and there was no talking until Pa had finished carving and sat down and tucked the big white napkin into his vest.

"There has been so much excitement," Ma said, "that we've not had time to talk about the post."

"Was it a good post?" Alec asked. They all knew that by "good" he meant, Was all the business taken care of?

"Moderately good," Pa said. "The cooper we expected writes he'll not come because his family will not live in such a wild place as he's heard this is. The world's full o' such fops and weaklings. I'll find a cooper in San Francisco or Portland and bring him back wi' me."

They all knew what a disappointment this was for Pa. And besides, it meant that until Pa could hire a cooper Gregory would have to do the cooper's work because he was the only one handy with the frow. Greg would have to work long hours making the staves for next season's barrels. With the new boathouse to build, there would be more work than even the stout Monroe boys could handle unaided. If there had ever been a chance for Greg to go south, Florence knew it was gone now.

Gregory looked down the table at Pa. "There's a cooper at Klawok village," he said. "That's not far away. Perhaps we could get him to come here and make staves for a couple of months."

"Gregory," said Pa, "how ye can make such outlandish proposals is more than a mon of guid sense can comprehend. I know this Klawok cooper as well as you do. He's a squaw man and you know it. I'll not have such riffraff on this beach, and ye know that too, as well as I do."

Greg's face flushed with anger. "The man has settled in this country and he's respectable. What if he is married to an Indian woman? Who else is there to marry?"

"And I suppose ye'll hold it couldn't be *this* squaw man who came to the village with spirits yesterday?" Pa's voice was hard and Florence cringed, wishing he would stop. "Ye had better watch yourself, Gregory. I'll have no such talk in this house."

Greg laid down his knife and fork as though to leave the table. Ma held up her hand. "Let us have peace," she said with her quiet dignity. "Let us not quarrel about a cooper."

There was a silence. Then Alec cleared his throat. "Was there word about the boat?" he asked, looking at Pa.

"Aye," said Pa. "The Company writes she'll be in on her trip this month as we expected."

For the remainder of the meal the talk concerned the shipping out of the salmon pack at Hunter Bay and Pa's purchasing trip south. The urgency for Jaimy and Alec to get supplies to the missionaries at Howkan made the meal brief, and Florence, longing for her letters, was glad of this. Finally, when they had all risen from the table, Pa reached in his pocket and drew out three letters, which he handed to his daughter.

"Let us hear what your young mon has to say," he said. "Is he coming along to go to San Francisco wi' me?"

Florence's heart leapt as she actually got the letters in her hand. "Thank you, Pa," she said. She had waited a month for these letters. She wanted to read them alone. "I'll help Ma clear," she said, "then I'll read them."

Before Pa could speak there came a knock at the front door. The Monroes stared at each other in amazement. There had never been such a knock before. One always heard or saw arrivals and stood with the door open. Laura darted for the door.

"Come back here, Miss," Pa ordered. But it was too late. She had already pulled the door wide open and stood beaming at a stocky, sandy-haired man.

Pa marched to the door and there was no welcoming smile on his face. With one look at him Ma caught hold of Laura and forced a retreat to the kitchen.

"Ye'll have the decency to get off my porch and off this beach," Pa said to the man.

Florence saw the expression of outrage on the man's face, saw the dark color rise from his neck to his forehead before he turned away. In this country where every door was open to the rare passer-by she saw Pa step out on the porch and close the Monroe door after him. She saw Pa speak to him and point out through the Narrows. The man turned on Pa defiantly, then just stared at him and shrugged and walked down to his skiff. There were tools and bundles in the skiff and in the stern an Indian woman sat quietly waiting.

Greg started for the door and Florence caught his sleeve. "Don't, Greg. It will only make Pa mad."

"How do you suppose that man's feeling?" Greg asked bitterly. "That's the cooper from Klawok. He's a decent man but to Pa he's no different than the rum seller who came yesterday."

Alec said, "Mind your tongue, Greg. Pa cannot do otherwise. You've got to draw the line somewhere."

"The one who came yesterday came in a dugout," Florence said, watching the man push off in the skiff. He rowed standing up facing the bow and he didn't once look around as the skiff went out through the Narrows.

"Oh, what's the use!" Greg said, pulling away from her. Without another word he went out through the kitchen and along the walk to the store.

Florence waited until the *Laura M.* had started off to the rescue of Howkan and the house was quiet again. Then she went to her room and sat by the window to read her letters. Beldon's letters were so full of his own charm. He said such lovely things, things that no one in the Monroe family, except perhaps Greg, would understand. He wrote little verses praising her beauty and he told her how radiant she was in his thoughts. The last of his letters gave her even more news than she had hoped for and put her troubled world in order again.

Dearly Beloved,
Since first you made me prisoner with a glance I have been waiting to write this letter to you. The

long exile is at an end and we can tell your father
that our future home is assured. I am living in my
dreams until I see you. Yesterday we loaded the
Lady Grace—you remember Father's schooner. We
loaded 350 barrels and 1000 half-barrels of sockeye
to bring the highest price on the market!

This news was almost beyond believing! Why,
in only one year—in his first year—Beldon had built
his saltery and packed almost as much salmon as
Pa and the boys. Avidly, she read on.

Father sailed out on the tide this morning and I shall
stay only long enough to finish weatherproofing the
house we built. As I sit here and look about it, I
know it is not worthy to shelter its future mistress!
My dearly Beloved, I shall build a castle for you some
day. But this little cabin will be snug and warm—
humble as it is—and you will grace it and give it
beauty such as no cabin ever had. I am coming to
Klinkwan in the sloop and bringing my cooper with
me in the hope that Mr. Monroe will have work to
keep him busy until my return from the States. We
shall leave soon and hope to have a few days with
you before the boat arrives at Hunter Bay. Perhaps
I shall be there before this letter!

The thought of seeing you makes it almost impossible to write. You are ever in my heart and I lay my
humble love at your feet.

Your devoted
Beldon Craig

With swimming eyes Florence ran downstairs. "Oh, Ma, he's coming—he'll be here just any day now. And Ma! He's bringing his cooper. I must tell Pa, and Greg."

As she ran out of the door Laura said, "I don't see why there should be such a fuss about a cooper."

CHAPTER 6

THE weather held for the next few days and in the Monroe house the excitement of anticipation was in the air. Florence stood often at the window, looking out through the Narrows, and Laura appointed herself official watcher and took up a station on Our Point. When the boys returned from Howkan and went again to Hunter Bay to wait for the boat, Laura considered it a time of such "important waiting" that frequently she had to be reminded that there were still the household duties to do. A day or two after the boys returned, the Indians began to come back to the village and the feasting and the house-building began again. But the same

spirit was not there and the noise was less. Young
Paul blamed the interruption and said it was the
white man's bad luck. Konutkan, the oldest nephew
of Yelthnow, brought a fresh-killed deer to Pa as
indemnity for the misbehavior that occurred the
day Florence was alone, but Young Paul was surly
and did not appear at the choir practice on Sunday.

Gregory tried to warn Pa that there was more to
this than appeared on the surface. "Young Paul is
ambitious," he said. "He would like to see himself
chief when Old Yelthnow dies. You watch—he'll try
to gain prestige enough to oust Konutkan."

Pa said, "Nonsense. Konutkan is sober and far-
seeing. He's Yelthnow's rightful heir and he'll be
chief when the old fellow dies."

Greg said no more, but Florence was uneasy and
wished that Pa would listen to him. She hadn't
thought what might happen when Old Yelthnow
died, as some day he must. It was Pa's agreement
with the old chief that kept everything in harmony
—the Yelthnow policy, as it were, that made the Indians friendly. But Pa believed that they would
soon be converted and that their heathen days were
numbered. He refused to believe that the power of
the medicine man might become a political aid for
Young Paul. The strain between Pa and Gregory
had grown so sharp of late that they seemed not to
agree on anything.

On the fifth day after the Howkan fire the
weather changed. You could tell it before the

clouds began to appear, by the little flurries of wind
and the haze on the south horizon. The swells in
the bay deepened and the surf rose high and white
on the rocky shores of the outer islands. Florence
spent the morning running to the windows, looking
to see if Beldon's sloop was in sight. She saw the
clouds begin to gather and travel in from Dixon
Entrance and she knew a southeaster was brewing.

As the day wore on and the overcast sky darkened she grew apprehensive lest Beldon be caught
by the storm before he could get through the Barrier Islands. Her face became anxious and grave
and Ma, coming downstairs from her afternoon nap,
stopped and put her arm around her daughter's
slender waist. Together they stood watching, silent
in the comfort of their mutual understanding. The
anxiety of waiting had become part of their lives
because it was they, the women, who were always
watching; watching for the *Laura M.* to come with
the mail or for the boys to come from Hunter Bay;
watching for Pa to return from a trip to Wrangell
or for the boat to come in from the sea. Florence
thought that when she married Beldon she would
never let him go away without her. She would go
with him wherever he went. She stood watching
the low line of mist driving in across the bay and
she knew the storm would soon be upon them.

The back door slammed and Laura came running
through the house. "Ma, can I pick the strawberries
before it rains?" she panted.

"*May* I," Ma corrected.

"May I?" Laura repeated quickly.

"Yes, dear, of course. Take the basket and pick only the ripe ones."

When Laura was gone, Ma sighed. "I think Pa will take her south with him and leave her with Cousin Liz. She's such a mite! But she is in need of the advantages of proper schooling."

"You always think of what's best for others," Florence said. "How can you be so brave? You know you'll miss Laura awfully if she goes." She kissed Ma on the cheek. "All I can think of is this wretched storm! Will Beldon get through the islands in time—or will he have to pull in somewhere? Oh, Ma, I hate this eternal waiting!"

Already the storm clouds had darkened the room and she turned impatiently from the window and went to the stove to put a match to the paper. The high spirits that had sustained her all day dwindled with the approaching storm, and disappointment that Beldon had not come was already creeping into her heart.

"Darling, we are not born patient. Patience is divine and we must earn it," Ma said. She came and put her arm through Florence's. "Let's go and make the tea," she said. "It's the watching that gets on your nerves."

Together they went to the kitchen to put fresh wood in the range and open the drafts. By the time they had set the kettle on to boil the fine rain began to blow into the cove. Florence thought of the heavy seas that would be breaking through the Barrier Islands and she began to fear for Beldon. Preoccupied and silent, she took the tea canister down from the shelf.

The door opened and Laura burst in, her golden curls powdered with the fine rain and her face shining. "Look!" she cried, showing her basket. "I got all of them, just in time."

Ma cried, "Mercy, child, why didn't you come in and get your rain cape?" She took the basket and looked at the shining wet strawberries. "They're beautiful," she said. "Now run up and put on your plaid and be sure to shake out your dress when you take it off."

"I'll keep a lookout while I'm dressing," Laura assured Florence as she ran out of the room.

Florence buttered the bread in silence. The tide-ridden coast was dangerous in a storm and Beldon would try to make it—she knew that. He would try to make it even if he were not going south with Pa. But it was important, she kept reminding herself, for him to be in time to meet the boat. It was his first business trip to see the shipping company in San Francisco and to make purchases for his saltery, a saltery that would produce as much as Pa's own next year. It was important that nothing should stand in his way, because next year she would be with him at Thorne Bay. They would be the Craigs of Thorne Bay. She paused in her buttering and

stared out through the kitchen window. Let nothing happen to him, she prayed silently. It's better
for him to be late for the boat. It's better for him to
lie in harbor somewhere than to risk his life. She
began to be panicky now, fearing that Beldon
would be reckless of the danger.

Then they heard Laura calling down the stairs.
"Beldon's coming! I see the sloop, the *Osprey!* He's
here!" Her voice was pitched high with excitement.

Florence dropped her knife and flew through the
dining room to the front window. Now that he had
actually come, after all the waiting and watching,
she was stunned with surprise. Had he really made
it? Had he really got here? As she pulled back the
curtain the color rose to her cheeks and faded and
rose again.

There in the Narrows was Beldon's sloop, with
the rain and the mist coming over her like puffs of
steam. Breathless, she watched her coming into the
wind, watched the sails flutter down. She saw Beldon spring forward with the light certainty of foot
and the sure movement that she remembered.
Eager and half-smiling, she watched his every
movement as he anchored the sloop in the channel
off the north point. She hardly saw the big man
who was with him, the cooper. With an excited
little "Oh!" she threw open the front door and waved
her handkerchief.

Beldon pulled off his sou'wester and held it up in
salute and the fine rain swept over his blond head.

Florence fluttered her handkerchief joyously and
then she bethought herself. With her hands up to
her hair, she turned and ran back into the house
past Ma. "Oh, I do look a fright," she exclaimed.
"I'll run up and change." Holding the front of her
skirt with both hands, she sailed up the stairs.

In her room she paused at the window and
watched the men on the sloop launching the tiny
white dinghy. She saw Gregory leave the store and
go down the beach to meet them, bareheaded, heedless of the rain. Hurriedly, she unbuttoned the
waist of her green twill and unfastened the skirt
and let it drop down around her feet. Then, in her
long flounced underskirt and embroidered corset
cover, she ran across the hall to wash her face and
neck with Ma's rose soap. When Ma came up she
had got into her blue foulard, wriggling her arms
through the long tight cuffs and reaching behind to
hook the hidden placket. Flushed and excited, she
was struggling with the many little buttons that began at her waist in the back and went all the way
up to her neck.

"Let me button you up." Ma's competent fingers
went at the buttons and in a moment she was done.
"Now smooth your hair, dear. You do look sweet
in blue."

As they descended the stairs she heard Gregory's
voice. "Oh, come *in*, Bel. We're used to dripping
coats and wet boots. Florence has been watching
for you all day. We all have. Come in."

But Beldon had stopped on the porch to pull off his oilskin coat and he was persisting in his attempt to stamp the water off his long gum boots.

With sedate speed little Ma reached the door ahead of Florence. "Oh, Beldon!" she cried, extending her hands. "We're so happy to see you. Gregory, take Beldon's coat and hang it in the shed to drip. Don't mind your boots, Beldon. Do come in."

At once shy and eager, Florence stood on the flowered carpet in the dim light of the hall. Whatever light there was seemed to have settled on the smooth roll of red hair at her neck and on the shining curls above her white forehead. Beldon Craig's blue eyes looked past Ma and Greg and in his glance she felt at once the salute and the obeisance of love. She stood in a trance of realization, knowing how perfect he was, how everything that he did was the perfect and only thing to do.

Gregory went past her with the wet oilskin. "Wake up, Cinderella," he grinned.

Then Beldon was there beside her, catching her two hands in his and looking into her eyes so deeply that she was aware of nothing except his gaze. Into the enchanted moment came Laura's footsteps, running up the hallway, shrinking those expanding seconds to the undistinguished tick of the big clock behind her. Beldon was looking at her with wonder and happiness in his eyes. "I thought I remembered," he said, "but you are lovelier than all my

dreams, sweeter than any thought," and he kissed
her hands—right in front of Ma.

Laura bit off the words that were on her lips and
stood staring at Beldon with wide, solemn eyes.

Ma said, "Come, Laura, help me bring in the tea.
Beldon must be chilled right through."

Reluctantly, Beldon turned to Laura, and Florence stood with her hands clasped together, still
feeling the warmth of his.

Beldon bowed to Laura. "Greetings, my lady,"
he said. "I've brought you something for your col-
lection."

"Oh, have you?" Laura cried. "Do let me see."

"Hold out your hands," he directed, and as she
made a cup with her hands he filled them with shining garnets extracted from his pocket. "They come
from up near Wrangell," he told her. "Some pros-
pectors found them."

Laura gazed at the stones. "Are they *jewels?*"
she asked, her voice filled with awe.

He nodded with mock seriousness. "Semipreci-
ous gems," he said.

Ma said, "Come now, Laura. We must get the
tea on." This time she steered her young daughter
toward the kitchen.

Florence went ahead of Beldon into the sitting
room, feeling so shy that she dared not look at him.
The room was in deep shadow now and the fire
shone brightly through the isinglass windows of the
Franklin stove. She walked across to it and opened

the doors to let the firelight out. "Was the summer long—very long?" she asked, still not looking at him.

"I don't know," he answered, slowly. "I—I wasn't there."

He stood gazing at her, the firelight touching his blond, curly hair and his sensitive mouth. His gaze was so like a caress that when she looked at him she blushed and had to look away again.

"But you wrote that it was long," she said, not understanding.

In the little pause they could hear the prolonged rushing sound of the rising wind.

"Yes," Beldon said. "I did. I did write that the summer was long. But now—why, just now—it seemed that you were standing on the steps with the early sun bright on your hair, as it was that day when I went away. And now it is raining and we have come in by the fire." Beldon stepped to the other side of the stove where he could see her face. "If the summer went by—between the sun and the rain—it went by like a shadow in which I couldn't exist—because you were not with me."

Florence raised her eyes to meet his. "Between the sun and the rain," she said softly. Her heart was singing with happiness. "I cannot even imagine your being away again," she whispered.

He looked at her face and her small ear with the little curled tendril of hair in front of it. "You are a flower," he said, "that the winter cannot touch, because I shall keep you in my heart."

He had taken a tiny box out of his pocket and he was holding it in his lean young hands as he tenderly removed the lid. "My mother sent this for me to give to you," he said. "If you'll look up, I'll show you what it is."

When she looked up she found him smiling and she smiled too, and murmured, "Oh, Beldon, how sweet of her to send this for me."

He was holding a little bowknot made of a ribbon of gold, and he pinned it on the velvet ribbon tied under her chin.

She could not speak because tears welled up in her eyes and she couldn't stop them, swept over as she was with happiness. Looking down, she put her hand over the little pin and her tears fell and splashed on the back of her hand.

There was a sound of steps in the hall. Gregory came in with his house slippers in his hand. "Oh, I say, I'm sorry," he said, apologetically, standing hesitantly, as though he would retreat if he could.

Florence looked up, startled to find that the room had got quite dark save for the firelight. "Goodness!" she said with a little catch of her breath. "I forgot to light the lamps! Come in and help, won't you, Greg?" She felt lightheaded, suspended in happiness so that nothing seemed quite real, and she behaved automatically.

Greg came into the room. "I didn't mean to intrude," he said, still embarrassed, "but I thought you'd want to get those boots off, Bel. They're devilish uncomfortable in the house!"

As Florence lighted the table lamp and replaced its round flowered shade, she lingered over the adjustment of the wick and when she looked up in the soft light she was composed again.

Beldon said, "Thanks, Greg. I should have brought my own house shoes in but I didn't think of it at the time."

Florence stood at the window as he pulled off his gum boots and got into Greg's slippers and she watched the first heavy squall rush in over the cove to slap rain across the panes and go roaring on into the forest.

"You just missed it, Bel," Greg said, coming to the window to stand beside her.

Beldon followed and they all stood looking out. "The southeaster! Harbinger of winter," said Greg, watching the wind-lashed cove foam white even within the protection of its points. "The poet's wind—in a land where no poet could live." He gave a bitter laugh, looking toward the totem poles standing dark and prophetic in the rain. Then he turned impulsively to Beldon. "Why don't you take Florence away from here, Bel? Why, in Heaven's name, do you want to stay in this rain-soaked wilderness?"

They hadn't heard Ma come until the china tinkled on the tray in the door. "Why, Gregory!" she said, reprovingly. "How can you call this a wilderness?" She looked around the comfortable room and then at her son.

Greg hastened to take the tray. "I didn't expect you to hear that," he said. "You mustn't mind me. I'm one of the monsters on the Monroe totem pole." He put the tray on the table and pulled a chair up for Ma. When she was seated he stood for a moment with his hands on the back of her chair, looking down at her neat head. "You mustn't mind me," he said again and turned to go out of the room. "I'll tell Pa and the cooper that tea's ready. They're talking in the store."

Beldon explained. "It's Einar Gren. I think you'll like him. He makes barrel staves faster than any man I ever saw. He's a big fellow and just as bashful as he is big."

"It's a better quality than boldness," said Ma. "We're glad to have Mr. Gren with us."

Laura came in, carrying two plates filled with bread-and-butter slices and cake squares. "It's a good thing you brought a cooper," she said. "There's no cooper around here except a squaw man and Pa threw him off the . . ."

"Laura," Ma said firmly, "will you please go to the kitchen and bring in some jam. It is not in good taste for little girls to engage in such conversation."

Florence was shocked by Laura's candid recitation of this embarrassing incident. She turned to the window to hide her confusion.

Ma said, "Laura is at a precocious age. I do hope

she will forget that dreadful word." With that said, she changed the subject. "You will find it interesting to visit San Francisco," she said to Beldon.

To their relief, Beldon followed her cue. "When we're in San Francisco I'll look in on the music stores," he said. "You would enjoy having some new songs, wouldn't you?"

"Oh, I'd love to have new music, Beldon. It's been ever so long since we saw a new song," Florence said. As she turned away from the window they heard the rumble of the *Laura M.'s* whistle.

"Mercy!" said Ma. "It must be the boys coming back."

Beldon cupped his hands around his eyes and peered out into the rain. "The boat must have got in before the blow," he said.

"If the boat's in they'll have the captain with them. He always comes to play the fiddle with Pa, you know, while she's loading." Ma was on her feet heading for the hall. "I'll get more cups," she said, and her voice was full of excitement. Ma loved company.

Florence and Beldon stood together, gazing out into the rain. If indeed the boat had come to Hunter Bay she would load the salmon and leave as soon as the weather permitted. Only the storm could prolong Beldon's stay.

C H A P T E R 7

7 HERE were three days of storm, with the seas combing the islands and riding into Cordova Bay to run themselves out against the islets protecting the cove of Klinkwan. The wind tore over the Monroe house, rattling its windows and slapping its tall frame with great invisible hands; the wind roared on through the forest, bending the young trees and whipping the old ones relentlessly until some of the giants fell crashing to the earth, unable to stand against the sweep of the southeaster. On the point the totems glistened darkly in the rain and the low Indian houses stood imperturbable as the wind whisked the smoke away from the roof vents as fast as it appeared.

The Monroe house stood against the storm, the lamplight shining at its many windows, but the excitement of the storm penetrated its walls. After the big supper the house rang with music and laughter when Pa cried, "The captain canna' leave until the storm's over. Come! We'll have some music and make merry his stay."

The captain of the boat was in no way saddened by his enforced stopover. He had been a friend of Ian Monroe before he ever came to Alaska. Alec brought his own violin downstairs for the captain to use and the two men tuned fiercely together and then played Scottish reels and songs until the table was cleared and the kitchen in order. Jaimy said to Florence in the kitchen that it sounded to him as though they were playing in competition with each other.

On the last night of the storm the singing took on a nostalgic tone, a sweet melancholy which stirred both memory and yearning in their hearts. Beldon stood all evening near the organ, watching Florence as she played, watching her hands on the keys and her eyes veiled with their long straight lashes. In the farthest corner of the big room Einar Gren, the cooper, sat like an enchanted giant. At the end of each solo he cried, "Bravo!" and then subsided, blushing, into his corner and would not come out and join them.

As the evening grew late Florence kept hoping that Gregory would sing *The Sea Mew* for Ma, for

all of them, because then it would be as it used to
be at home when the family would sit quietly in the
parlor of the big house in Victoria just to hear Gregory sing. She looked at him now, sitting over
against the wall, his eyes dark and brooding, and
she wondered what he was thinking. She looked
from him to Beldon, standing near her. Beldon was
slight of figure and graceful, like Greg, but he
was so fair and blue-eyed, so ready to smile. He was
like Greg in many ways but so different in mood.
Yet she loved them both more than any of the
others, more than anything else in the world—except
God and duty, she reminded herself sternly. Softly,
she began to play the opening chords of *The Sea
Mew.*

This was Ma's favorite song and Gregory was the
one to sing it. In a family of fine voices Gregory's
was the finest of all. As Florence played the lovely
melody he looked up at her and she gave him a
smile of entreaty. "Please," she said.

Greg got up and came and stood with his back
to the rain-swept windows behind her. In the
silence that fell upon the room, the roar of the wind
and the sea and the soft tones of the organ seemed
to blend. When Gregory sang, Florence could close
her eyes and see him standing on a great stage in
London with a real audience in front of him. Now
she felt the tragedy of his standing there between
the starched lace curtains with the storm lashing at

the windows behind him. She played softly, feeling poignantly the loneliness of the song.

Gregory began singing.

The stars are all burning cheerily, cheerily,
  Ho ro Mhairi dhu, turn to me!
The sea mew is mourning drearily, drearily,
  Ho ro Mhairi dhu, turn to me!

As he sang he stepped back and leaned against the wall, with his hands behind him and his eyes half closed. His voice had such range and power and he used it with such sensitive feeling that his audience became oblivious to all save the sweetness and loneliness of the song.

High up is his home, on the cliff's naked breast,
But warm is her plumage that blesseth his nest!
  The ice-winds ne'er blow there,
  And soft falls the snow there, oh!
Ho ro Mhairi dhu, turn to me!

No one moved after the last note. They all sat as if a spell had been cast upon them and none could move until some one of them said the magic word. Laura had been leaning on Ma's lap, watching Gregory as he sang. Now suddenly, she ran forward, flung her arms around him, and cried, "Oh, Greg, don't ever go away!" And the spell was broken.

He laughed and lifted her up, swinging her back
and forth like a pendulum. "Silly!" he said. "It's
you that's going away, not me."

Everyone began to talk, but still some of the enchantment remained in the room and there were
pauses when the talk stopped and the room was
quiet. More than once Ma said, "I do love it when
we are all together singing."

Gregory was exhilarated and lively, and he
plagued Beldon until he also contributed to the evening's entertainment. Beldon explained that he
couldn't carry a tune in a tub, and everybody
laughed when he half sang, half talked, "Clear the
kitchen, old folks, young folks." Greg made him do
it again while he himself sang a comic obligato and
the family rocked with laughter at the antics of the
two as they sang the verse.

> *A jay bird sat on a hickory limb.*
> *He winked at me, I winked at him.*

They went to bed laughing, and in the night the
wind blew itself out. The house was quiet after the
final squalls rushed over and went howling into
the dark forest behind it.

In the morning Ian Monroe called his family together in the big, cold sitting room. He put his
tweed cap on the table and stood there in his greatcoat. They all stood around him with serious faces
and that depressed feeling that comes with being

up too long without breakfast. Alec had already got the fire going in the *Laura M.* and Einar Gren was out there now, watching the steam gauge. The captain had insisted that his passengers and the boys eat breakfast on the boat at Hunter Bay, because he thought Ma and Florence should be spared the trouble of getting an early breakfast for all of them. He and Beldon were already taking the luggage out in the skiff.

Laura clung to Ma's arm, looking tense and uncomfortable. She wore the same traveling costume she had worn when she left Victoria almost a year and a half before and she had outgrown it considerably, so that the sleeves and the hem had had to be let down. Watching Pa from under her little bonnet, she seemed ready to bolt at any minute and fly to the safety of her own room. Jaimy stirred restlessly as he stood with his hands in his pockets, waiting. Gregory leaned with his arms on the back of a chair, looking speculatively at Alec, who stood upright with his hands at his sides, showing no feeling that the moment was important or that he was missing his breakfast. Florence wished that Pa would hurry and get it over with, because she hated departures. It would be a month before she would even have a letter from Beldon and all the long winter lay ahead.

Pa looked very brisk and handsome, with his beard freshly trimmed and his brown tweeds pressed. He looked around at them all and began with Alec. "Alec, I want ye to devote as much time as ye can to the boathouse. Get the studding up and the roof on as soon as ye can. Put Young Paul on to help. He'll be glad enough for work when his potlatch is done. After the boat leaves close up the saltery, but while I'm gone take a run over to Hunter Bay now and again to look at it."

Alec listened and nodded. "I'll see to it all, Pa," he said.

Pa went on to Greg. "Gregory, ye'll help the boys bring the freight back from the saltery—and, mind ye, check the manifests carefully. Get the goods in order on the shelves and keep the store open for a day or two until the Indians have made their purchases. Then I want ye to make shakes for the roof of the boathouse. Let nothing interfere wi' that."

He paused and his face grew stern as he looked at Gregory. Florence glanced nervously at her gray-eyed brother, looking so silent and dark as he leaned on his chair near Jaimy.

"And, Gregory," Pa went on, "I'm going to warn ye for the last time that there'll be no familiarity with the Indians on the part of any member of this household. There are times when ye seem to forget you're a Monroe. It is painful to have to remind ye that the Indians stay in their village and the Monroes in this house."

Greg's face flushed and Florence could see his knuckles grow white where his hands gripped the back of the chair. He met Pa's look steadily but he said nothing. The moment stretched on painfully.

Finally Pa cleared his throat and continued. "Jaimy will work with Alec. Mr. Gren will work in the woods, and by the time ye have the roof on the boathouse he'll be ready to have ye help him bring the bolts down there where he'll have shelter to make the staves."

Pa stopped and looked at his wife. "Maggie, I've told ye about the blue flannel and the sewing machine. The boys will bring them here when they return with the freight. It will give Flossie and you a task to keep your hands busy and make the time fly."

"I'm sure it will," Ma said, but she looked doubtful.

Then Pa moved away from the table and bowed his head. He asked God to guard them all, to make plain to them their trespasses and to guide them in the way of their duty.

His parting from Ma was formal and Ma remained cheerful as she bade them all good-by, so that Laura wouldn't cry. Florence put on her wrap to go down to the water's edge with them but Ma remained at the window.

Outside, the air was full of mist drifting in from the sea. It came heaving and rolling across the wide bay and hung like a curtain of fine rain over the islands. The tide was out and yellow seaweed showed brightly on the points and on both sides of the Narrows. The tide was so low that the cove looked small, almost surrounded by its dark wet beach. Their feet crunched in the black shale as they went down the steep beach, Pa and the boys leading and Florence and Beldon following, with Laura between them. The captain was already at the skiff and he stood there, raising his hat to Ma where she stood at the window. Florence felt tight and wordless and, with Laura clinging to her hand, she was too shy to try to tell Beldon how sad she was at parting and how her every thought would be for him while he was gone.

"It's such a long way," she said, "such a long way to San Francisco."

"It's not far to Victoria, though, is it?" Laura asked anxiously.

"I'll tell you who knows how far it is," Beldon said. "Your brother Gregory knows. Scoot ahead there and ask him."

Laura ran after Greg, calling his name. Beldon took Florence's hand and tucked it under his arm. Florence clung to him, constrained and silent, knowing how she would miss him. When he spoke his voice was low and so full of emotion she thought it was going to break. "Don't be sad, my Florence, my dear. I shall keep you in my heart now—and always—even though the ocean be between us."

It seemed to Florence that the next moments went by in a streak of time that she tried to stop and could not. There they all were—everyone getting into the skiff except herself, and Beldon standing holding her hands, looking at her, with the mist settling on the fine ends of his curly hair.

Pa said, "Come along, lad! The winter will soon be over and you'll be home again."

Florence knew they had all been talking, but she didn't know what they had said. Laura was clinging to her skirts and she bent and kissed her. She was trembling and she let the child go quickly lest she perceive it. Then they were all in the skiff shouting good-bys to Ma, and the water was widening between her and Beldon.

Pa called, "Watch over your Ma, Flossie. She'll need ye."

Jaimy yelled that they would be in with the supplies on the high tide tomorrow because the evening tide would be too late. Alec cautioned her not to forget to get the storeroom ready, and suddenly Laura began to cry. Florence saw Beldon pick Laura up and hold her, pointing shoreward, and Laura seemed to be comforted. Because the tide was so low, it took no time for them to row out through the narrow entrance to the cove to where the *Laura M.* lay steaming and smoking in the channel. At the steamer they all turned and raised their hats to Ma at the window and to Florence, standing there on the beach. Tears welled up in her eyes and they swam mistily before her, but she stood watching, with Donny sitting behind her until they were ready to pull out. Then she realized that the tide had crept up around her feet and her shoes

were wet and that the Indian children playing on
the point were staring at her with solemn, interested
faces. She turned away and went desolately back
up the beach.

On the porch she turned again and watched the
Laura M. pulling out past Our Point with the blue
smoke pouring out of her tall, thin stack. In the
stern, shrouded in smoke and mist, Pa and Beldon
stood with their arms raised in salute. The *Laura
M.'s* whistle let out a rumble and Florence waved
her handkerchief until they were gone out of sight.

Ma opened the door. "Come in, dear, out of the
cold," she said. "How sweet Beldon was to watch
over Laura like that!"

Florence was too near tears to speak. She
nodded, trying to smile, and Donny followed her
in and pressed against her sympathetically.

Ma said, "You're cold, child. Run up and put on
your slippers and your cozy. We'll make tea in the
kitchen."

Upstairs in her cold room, Florence stood by the
window for a moment, looking out. There was
nothing to tell that the *Laura M.* had been there,
but Beldon's sloop lay quietly at anchor and the
sight of it brought a little glow of comfort to her.
Beyond it fog wreathed the little islands, and mist
rose from among the trees like smoke drifting up to
heaven. The gulls flying high over the cove glided,
ghostlike, in and out of the mist. The totem poles,
wet and dripping, stared blankly across the cove at

the drooping cedars on Our Point and behind them
the village still slept. Only the children were out.
Everywhere, far and near, was the small wet sound
of trickling water. Florence gazed at Beldon's sloop
and her heart began to ache with waiting before
the waiting had begun.

CHAPTER 8

*Y*OUNG PAUL'S friends finished building his house the day Pa went away. It was the first house in the village to have a stovepipe and more than two windows. It stood at the end of the village, looking raw and up-to-date and out of place behind its handsome new totem pole. The sky had cleared that evening and Ma and Florence watched the goings on in front of Paul's house from the window in Gregory's room.

Paul and his wife distributed the blankets from the front porch of the new house. They gave away two hundred blankets and Paul became so exalted with his own importance that he swaggered about, talking too much. He pointed toward his totem pole and to the store as though both belonged to him, and neither Ma nor Florence could figure out what he was talking about. When darkness fell and the Indians went again to the community house of Yelthnow to dance, Ma and Florence went to bed. The day had been long and they were tired from their efforts to be cheerful in each other's presence. They undressed in silence and slept side by side in Ma's big bed for their mutual comfort.

The next morning they woke apathetic and weary, after the rush of so much company and the strain of the departure. Ma was thoughtful as she laid her clothes along the edge of the bed and began to dress, the garments disappearing one by one under her voluminous gown. Florence gazed absently out of the window as she rolled her hair into a knot at the nape of her neck.

They made fires in the stoves downstairs and in Ma's room, too, because the nights were getting cold and Ma wanted to keep the damp out. They spent the morning getting the big storeroom at the end of the kitchen in order so that all would be ready when the boys came in with the supplies. Six months' supplies took a good deal of space and the matter of arrangement was important. Florence had finished cleaning the two bins where rice and beans were to be stored, when she heard the voices of the Indians on the walk outside. She climbed up on the meat block to peer through the little diamond-

shaped window that lighted the storeroom and saw
Young Paul coming along the walk. It seemed to
her that all the visitors and some of the men of the
village were with him. They walked past the store
and came on toward the house.

She climbed down and rushed into the kitchen.
"Ma! Ma!" she cried. "Young Paul's coming over
here and he's got them with him. All those wild
strangers are with him!"

Ma said, "Now don't get excited, dear. Our Indians have always respected Pa, and Old Yelthnow
will see to it that the visitors behave themselves."

But even while Ma was talking the Indians had
reached the house and thick at the windows she
could see the painted faces peering in. There came
a thumping at the door.

Florence felt the color leave her face. "What shall
we do, Ma?" she asked, trying to fight down her
fear.

Ma made a brief, uncertain movement; then she
started for the door. "I'll go to the door, of course,"
she said. "We must keep our dignity."

Florence started after her. "I'll go, Ma. Let me
go."

"Sit down, dear, please," Ma said. "It's my place
to go."

McDuff made a dash under the stove as Ma
opened the door. Donny followed her, standing
close behind her, alert and watchful. Florence sat
down as Ma had asked her to do, but she sat on the

edge of the chair. From the tail of her eye she
could see the movement at the windows above the
sink and suddenly she was angry. Here she was,
sitting like a scared bird while Ma faced them all.
She got to her feet and went about the kitchen
chores without so much as a glance at the windows.
She heard Young Paul's voice, a little louder than
was natural, as though he thought Ma a little deaf.

"I paint house," he was saying. "You open store,
please. I buy paint."

Ma looked Paul in the eye. "Mr. Monroe would
not be pleased if he saw you come here, Paul," she
said. "My sons will be back soon. They will open
the store."

Paul was the only one in the crowd who could
speak or understand English. He stood there with
a perfectly bland expression on his face and said,
"My friends come long way. They go soon. I want
paint now."

"I don't think you mean to be impertinent," said
Ma. "My sons come soon. You go now and wait."
She spoke firmly and closed the door.

Outside, the Indians began jeering at Young Paul.
He had gone too far, they could see, and now they
were making fun of him. Then, over the confusion
of their voices, came the voice of a woman speaking
Haida very fluently and angrily. It was a magnificent voice, deep and vibrant as an organ; it was a
voice that Florence recognized. The men moved
away from the windows and their talk and jeering

stopped. They all shuffled about in embarrassment
and confusion, stepping off the boardwalk into the
deep grass and jostling each other as they made for
the village. Watching from the windows, Florence
and Ma saw the wife of Old Yelthnow coming along
the walk scolding as she came. She did not stop
until she was at the door of the Monroe kitchen. At
the door she turned and waved the men on with an
imperious gesture of her arms.

Ma left the window and opened the door. The
chief's wife stopped talking as abruptly as she had
begun and, turning to Ma, she sadly shook her head.
Ma held the door wide and with a gesture invited
the Indian woman in. She came in and sat on a
chair near the door, her hands folded in her lap and
her face grave and composed. It seemed to Florence that a tranquil melancholy descended upon
her and upon the room, a timeless sadness that
spoke more clearly than words. Ma drew a chair
away from the table and sat near Yelthnow's wife.
McDuff came and jumped into Ma's lap and she
stroked him. The two women sat there in silence.

Florence tiptoed away to the floor above to do
up the bedrooms. Everywhere there were vacant
spots where Laura's things had been. As she
smoothed the bed she found herself listening as
though she hoped to hear her sister's voice somewhere in the big house. But the house was silent
and she sighed and continued her work absently,
thinking of Beldon and of Pa and wondering if it

would always be her fate to suffer the loneliness of waiting.

The sound of the *Laura M.'s* whistle, followed by cries and shouts, broke in on her reverie and she hastened to the window. The boys had come from the saltery and the *Laura M.* was already at the point with the little scow in tow. The cove was brimming full now, with the tide almost up to the doorstep. Out in the channel Beldon's sloop rode quietly at anchor and everywhere the reflections were clear in the still water. The people of the village were gathered along the water's edge, watching the boys maneuver the scow in to the landing platform in front of the store. Eager and filled with curiosity, many of them launched their little dugouts and paddled out around the scow to get a closer look at the cargo. Among them Nakatla drove her own little dugout slowly through the water with easy strokes of the paddle as she circled around the *Laura M.* On the shore the children shrieked with delight and yelled back and forth until the cove was a bedlam of noise.

"Ma! They're here!" Florence cried, running down the stairs. In the dining room she remembered Yelthnow's wife and she slowed down and walked into the kitchen. The two women were still sitting there in silent dignity just as she had left them. When Florence came in, the old Indian woman rose, her many bracelets tinkling together on her arms. She walked to the door without attempting to speak.

Ma got up, letting McDuff slip to the floor, and opened the door. "Thank you," she said to her departing guest. "Thank you." She closed the door and they could see the top of Mrs. Yelthnow's head as she walked past the windows.

"The boys are home," Florence said, wondering if Ma had heard her call.

"Yes, dear," Ma said. "I was just thinking of Mrs. Yelthnow. She was very kind. It might have been quite—quite embarrassing, had she not come. She was very reassuring."

"Just the same, I'm glad the boys are home," Florence said. "And I'm glad Mr. Gren's going to be here all winter. It's lonely living with people you don't understand and who don't understand you."

"I know, dear," Ma said. "Sometimes I think how nice it would be if . . ." She stopped and laughed. "I'm woolgathering," she said. "Come, let's sit on the porch and watch the boys unload."

They took chairs to the front porch and sat there to watch the cove. Alec brought the *Laura M.* in slowly and all around him the Indians paddled this way and that in their dugouts, shouting and laughing with excitement. Jaimy was in the skiff and Einar Gren on the scow, which they made fast to the piling under the store with a line they put ashore. Then Alec backed the little steamboat away and ran it to the anchorage outside the points of the cove where Beldon's sloop was moored. On these big tides the water came right up under the store and filled the cove so that no beach showed at all. The totem poles were reflected on its smooth surface and at the head of the cove the Monroe house looked down upon itself in the tide not ten feet from its doorstep. Outside the entrance to the cove, Alec let off the steam in a great white plume that was reflected like a cloud on the water. He and Gregory came ashore in the dinghy, and Nakatla paddled along after them in her little dugout, talking to Gregory and smiling so that her fine white teeth showed.

Florence said, "Look, there's that girl, the one Greg always talks to."

"I'm sure he talks to all of them," Ma said. "He's interested in their language, you know."

"I wish he had been here this morning," Florence said. "I think he ought to know how Young Paul behaved."

They watched the Indians gather around Greg as he came ashore and they could see that he was giving directions concerning the unloading. Young Paul and Konutkan began to help the boys pull the crates and boxes up to the loading platform. Jaimy left the crowd and came walking through the tall beach grass along the edge of the water. He stopped below them with one foot on the step. "How are the girls?" he asked, grinning up at them.

"Laura sent a million good-bys and Bel managed
to keep her cheerful right up to the time they pulled
out." Jaimy's heartiness subsided and he looked out
through the Narrows. "We watched the boat steam
away—out past the islands—south," he finished.

"My poor little Laura," Ma murmured. "I hope
she won't be too homesick."

"We're the ones to be homesick," Jaimy said.
Then he laughed again and looked at Ma. "I'm
only joshing," he said. "Where you are is home."
He looked at his sister. "Bel looked pretty glum,"
he told her. "He doesn't know when he's well off."

Ma said, "Now Jaimy, don't tease. Will you bring
our things over now or later on?"

"We're going to bring them now," Jaimy said.
"Then we'll all light in and help Greg get the stuff
on the shelves in the store. Better decide where you
want the sewing machine."

"Goodness me, I forgot all about it," Ma said.

When Einar Gren and Jaimy brought the first
load over on the hand truck, Ma and Florence were
ready for them. They unloaded the sewing machine
and wheeled it into the kitchen after the crate had
been knocked apart.

"I hope there's a book of lessons in it," Ma said,
looking at the spidery iron legs and the treadle.

"It's got little drawers," Florence cried, "and look,
a key!"

"Well, where do you want it?" Jaimy asked. He

came in and dropped a big bundle on the table. "This is the flannel, four bolts of it."

With a knife Florence ripped open the heavy paper wrapping. There were four bolts of baby-blue outing flannel. "Oh, Ma, the Indians will look simply awful in underwear made of that," she exclaimed. Then she remembered Mr. Gren standing in the doorway and she blushed and caught hold of the machine to hide her embarrassment. "I'll help you wheel it in," she said to Jaimy.

Ma explained quickly. "Mr. Monroe thinks they should wear undergarments. They don't, you know. Of course we must try to sew them. It may be in a good cause after all."

"Yes, ma'am," Mr. Gren agreed. "It sure will."

Load after load of supplies was brought to the kitchen and Florence worked industriously, stowing them away in the storeroom. She hung hams and sides of bacon along the stout hooks in the ceiling. Together, she and the others stowed tins of fruit and vegetables, milk, and meat on the shelves. Jaimy and Mr. Gren lugged in hundred-pound sacks of flour, sugar, and meal. The barrels of butter and the eggs in water glass were stored in the shed outside, and the sacks of green coffee beans brought in and put in the darkest corner. Little crocks of cheese and marmalade were put down near the floor where it was cool, and the nutmegs and whole spices had a box of their own. The sacks of salt were put up high with the dried fruit, and the pails

of lard on the floor. When everything was in there
was not a foot of space left unfilled in the big storeroom. Ian Monroe was a good provider.

That night Ma tried to persuade Einar Gren to
stay with them in the house. "We're used to so
many," she explained. "You would be no trouble
at all."

But the big cooper backed up against the wall,
looking huge and awkward as though she had him
cornered, and tried bashfully to tell her that he did
not doubt her hospitality but that it was his job to
live on Beldon's sloop and take care of it.

It wasn't until after supper that there was time to
talk about anything. Ma took one look at the sewing machine and said, "We'll leave that until tomorrow." They had put it in the dining room
because the table was there to cut out on. They
went on to the sitting room, both of them missing
Laura, because this was the time of day when she
had helped most with the chores and it had been
quiet in the kitchen without her. In the sitting room
Gregory sat at the organ, playing softly, and Florence was surprised, because he had done it so seldom of late. Jaimy was reading the newspapers the
captain had given them and Alec sat in Pa's chair
reading the Bible. Ma took her darning basket and
sat down in her rocking chair near the lamp, and
Florence took a chair to the organ and sat close to
Gregory.

"Something happened this morning I think you

should know about," Ma said, and all the boys looked at her because she so seldom commanded their attention. She told them about the incident of Young Paul and of Yelthnow's wife.

Alec was the first to respond. "Young Paul knows better than that," he said. "Do you know anything about this?" he asked Greg.

Greg stopped pumping, but his hands were still on the keys. "It's the last day of his potlatch. He thinks he's a pretty big fellow now," he explained. "He was trying to show that he could get what he wanted when he wanted it. It was stupid of him— he isn't stupid ordinarily." He began playing the organ again, softly.

"I'll speak to Yelthnow tomorrow," Alec said.

"Oh, I wish you wouldn't," Ma said. "Mrs. Yelthnow was very kind and she understood, I'm sure, that Young Paul was overstepping himself."

"I don't think Paul will do that again," Greg said. "He wants influence in the village and the very fact that you didn't let him bluff you will make him more careful."

Ma picked up her darning. "I do hope he won't make any trouble with Pa away."

"Young Paul will have to learn to behave himself," Alec said. "If we let one slip go by, there'll be another. Tomorrow I'll speak to him."

Alec sounded so much like Pa that no one in the room said anything. There was only the sound of Gregory's music.

CHAPTER 9

AFTER the departure it took the family quite a little time to get settled down again. Ma was resolutely cheerful; but the table seemed so big, she said, with both Pa and Laura away. From Pa's chair at the head Alec agreed that it was quiet with the little nipper gone, and Jaimy mimicked Florence's lovelorn gaze every time he caught her dreaming. Gregory spent more time with them all and he talked more and laughed more. Even when he said that perhaps Laura had escaped for good and would never come back to this Godforsaken wilderness, his voice was less bitter than it used to be.

The boys and Einar Gren spent days in the woods

felling the big spruce trees and sawing them into
stave lengths, while at home Florence and Ma
struggled with the blue outing flannel. In Victoria
there always had been a seamstress who came to do
the sewing each year and, while Ma had taught
Florence to embroider and hemstitch and to mend
lace, neither of them had ever "sewed garments."
They finally got under way by making a pattern
from a pair of Pa's underdrawers, but it took considerable studying before they dared to lay the scis-
sors to the flannel. Finally, with the yards of blue
stuff spread out on the big dining-room table, Florence cut out the legs and Ma basted them. At the
end of a week they had a goodly number made and
they tried to fit them together. It was then they
discovered that they were all right legs and when
they fitted them together they had half a seat before
and half a seat behind. They couldn't be turned
and matched up because the outing flannel was
smooth on one side and fluffy on the other. After
the shock of this discovery wore off and it was seen
that there was ample flannel left to correct the mistake, Ma laughed until tears rolled out of her eyes,
while Florence hastened to cut out a left leg and
baste a pair together before proceeding.

By the end of October the days were growing
short and the mountains were capped with the first
fresh snow. There was a good spell of weather and
Florence launched the dugout on the far side of Our
Point and paddled among the islets, gathering wild

crab apples. Often she drifted with the tide in the little canoe, idle and dreaming. So great was her love that it included everything about her. The beauty and the solitude of the country became her own—hers and Beldon's—because they were young and the country would bend to their hearts. She gloried in the sun because soon the winter storms would be upon them. She felt no gloom at the prospect of winter; it would pass and then would come her wedding day.

When Alec and Jaimy fetched the letters from the Mission, letters from Victoria and San Francisco and from Astoria, where Beldon had gone to visit his own family, Florence read and reread her own, and they all read Laura's letters out loud. The letters made talk for them for days. Pa's letters told them that the wife of the president of the Company was assisting him in his shopping for the ladies at home and the two of them were arranging all the frills and furbelows for the wedding. He said he would be home before Christmas and the boys were to meet him in Wrangell early in December. With the reading of Pa's letter the work about the place accelerated for a few days as if Pa himself had appeared with new orders. The hammer blows fell faster in the boathouse, and the blue flannel legs became pairs ready to stitch on the sewing machine in no time.

There came a morning in the first week in November that dawned clear, with frost on the needles of the spruce trees and on the bending beach grass in front of the house. The salmonberry brush between the house and the store had turned deep red and the stems were yellow and dry, waiting for the wind that would leave them bare as sticks in winter. The late sun shone across the frosty roof of the Monroe house and cast its light on the figures atop the village totem poles, on the monstrous beak of the raven and on the ears of Yelthnow's wolf. In its slowly descending light each bear and eagle, each salmon and beaver and killer whale came, bright with color, out of the retreating shadow. Gregory had gone early to start the fire in the store, but he came back almost immediately with an Indian basket full of small dark-red berries.

Ma and Florence were still tidying up the kitchen and old Mary's broom could be heard in the front hall.

"Here's a present," Greg said, smiling at Ma, "basket and all. Nakatla—you know, the one who taught me Haida—she sent them to you."

"Why, they're wild cranberries," cried Ma. "Where did she get them, Gregory? I haven't seen such since we first came to Canada, years ago. Where do they pick them, Gregory? They make good sauce, you know."

"I'll find out where they grow," Greg said. "Do you want to pick some yourself?"

"Oh, *do* let's!" Florence coaxed. "Let's go and pick more. We can take a picnic lunch. It's such a lovely day and there may not be another with winter so near. And Ma, you haven't been out for ages."

"But Florence, dear, we haven't planned," Ma objected weakly.

Florence could see that she really wanted to go. It was only the surprise that had taken her aback. "Let's give ourselves a surprise," she teased. "I'll dash out and ask Alec. Greg, you'll find out where the berries grow right away, won't you?"

Without giving him time to reply, she ran out of the door and over to the boathouse to ask Alec.

It was seldom that anything was undertaken in the Monroe family without due consideration and planning, but this morning Florence's exuberance was so great, and so eager was she to get away from the house and the blue flannel, that even Alec was carried away. He agreed to spare Jaimy for the day, not forgetting to warn him to keep an eye out for bears and to see to it that Ma was never out of his sight.

From the Indians Greg learned that the cranberries grew only in the muskeg and that there was a muskeg swamp around the point to the north where they grew in great quantity. "The old Indians are superstitious about the place and won't go near it," he said. "The young ones laugh when they tell you about it—but you couldn't bribe one of them to go there, just the same." After the flurry of getting ready he walked with them down to the skiff where

Jaimy waited. "Nakatla says that she's been there once and the berries are thick," Greg told them.

He helped them in and pushed the skiff off. "Keep an eye out for the spirits and monsters." He laughed. "And bring your pails home full." He stood waving as they started rowing out, laughing and joking about the haunted swamp.

Florence was at the forward oars and Jaimy in the middle. In the stern Ma sat with a blanket over her knees and a big black umbrella to protect her face from the flashing reflection of sun on the water. In the bow were Jaimy's rifle, the lunch basket and berry pails, and Donny, looking ahead and eagerly sniffing the air.

"Florence dear, try to keep the veil down on both sides of your hat," Ma cautioned. "This weather is so squinty."

But as they rowed out of the cove Florence leaned on her oars and let the veil blow, happy to be away from the confinement of the house and the prospect of work on the blue flannel underwear. "Oh, Ma," she objected, "the bright days will soon be over. Even Jaimy's freckles will bleach out by Christmas."

They rowed around the *Laura M.* to get out of the cove and on past Beldon's sloop, anchored at the point, and out through the Narrows. Then they turned north, taking the channel between the Indian burial point and an island farther offshore. The burial point curved down toward the village from the north, where it was attached to the shore by a neck of land that was covered with water at flood tide. As they rowed along the farther side of this high-tide island they could see the Indian graves with their totems and fences, the great carved eagles and bears timeless and quiet in the sun. They rowed north around the low elbow of the point and, keeping inside the tiny islets, they could look between them to the mouth of Klakas Inlet. All around them the water danced in the breeze, flashing and alive. On this side of the point, with the hill out of the way, they could see the wild mountains with snow on their tops. They were not high mountains but they were rugged, separate peaks, with great gorges, streams, and muskeg swamps between them. They were lonely mountains, leaning away from each other so that they gave no sweep of direction.

Ma's big umbrella protected her from the view of the lonely mountains, and her eyes dwelt upon the inviting little islets standing above their quivering reflections of autumn color. "My, it's pretty," she said, smiling out from under the umbrella.

Jaimy described the place where they were to land. "There's a crick runs out, Greg said, and beyond that we pull in. The shore line here faces north and the woods are clear of brush except along the crick."

As they drew in near the shore, looking for the creek, the skiff slid into the dark green shadow of the rocky shore line where the forest grew down to the very limit of the tide. They had rowed well over a mile, going easily with the flooding tide, when they saw the creek. At its mouth the devil clubs and wild currants grew jungle-like and the dark stream, red with the muskeg stain, gushed forth past the green foliage and tumbled noisily into the salt water. A few yards beyond it they found a small V-shaped beach between the dark rocks, and here they pulled in. Above the beach the forest floor came out like a bench, ending abruptly, with twisted roots and root tendrils hanging out over the shale where the storm tides had beaten the earth away. As they got out of the skiff the trees towered dark and silent above them, casting a heavy shadow on the beach and the water at its edge. A cold breath blew out of the forest, smelling of fungus and mold. Out beyond the shadow the water quivered and danced in the sun, sending up bright explosions of light.

Florence looked into the forbidding gloom of the forest and then out again to the bright islands. "Don't the cranberries grow anywhere else?" she asked. "This is such a cold place."

"They only grow in muskeg swamps," Jaimy said. "Across in Klakas Inlet you get a southern exposure and it's warmer, but it's too far to row and besides, that's where the Indians pick." He tied a rock about a third of the way down the skiff's painter and then he set the rock on the bow tip and pushed the skiff

out into deep water. "We're explorers," he laughed.
"I'll bet there's never been human foot set on this
beach until now." He jerked the painter, and the
rock fell off and sank, anchoring the skiff where she
wouldn't ground when the tide turned. He made
fast the end he was holding and picked up his rifle.

Ma reached out her hands to let them help her
over the roots. "I'm sure the Indians are very wise
in avoiding this place," she said. "But now that we
are here we mustn't go back with our pails empty."

"They have funny beliefs," Jaimy said, "but I
don't think their demons will chase us." He started
into the dim woods, walking slowly so that Ma
could keep up without exertion. Donny ran in
circles around them, sniffing and watching, running
ahead out of sight and then dashing back to find
them again. Jaimy, calling him to stay close, shep-
herded them along, keeping the sound of the creek
to the right as his guide.

The spruce and hemlock here were giants. Scat-
tered among them, huckleberry bushes grew tall
and pale-green, reaching up for what little light
sifted down through the interlacing branches.
Looking ahead, Florence could see nothing but tree
trunks with their ghostly pale lichens and shelving
fungi. In the deep silence she strained her ears,
listening, and tried to still the rustle of her own
skirts. Underfoot the floor of the forest was springy
with centuries of fallen hemlock needles and the
tawny moss of the coastal hills. Above, the deep

green branches were empty of life and motionless, but the floor of the forest upon which she walked was crisscrossed with the narrow trails of the fur-bearing animals and the track of the timber wolf.

Ma took a quick glance around her. "My, it's spooky, isn't it?" she said, and her voice seemed small and lost in the magnitude of the trees.

Before Florence could reply there was a rush of sound overhead. Startled, they both looked up. The interlacing branches were motionless and so thick they couldn't see through them.

"Mercy!" cried Ma. "What's that?"

"Ravens," Jaimy replied, laughing. "They won't hurt you."

Then Florence recognized the sound, the sibilant sound of great wings beating the air. When the noise was past the silence seemed even deeper than before. They were going up an easy ascent. Jaimy led them around the moss-covered windfalls and used the animal trails when he could. Ma was quiet after hearing the flight of the ravens, and Jaimy teased her about the Indian superstition.

"I think it's strange," Florence said. "I don't know why, but it does seem sinister."

"Some places are like that," Ma said bravely. "The Celts claimed that evil little folk lived in places like this."

Presently ahead of them they could see the sunlight coming through the trees. It fell in spots of gold into the gloom of the forest. As the trees

thinned out there were fewer spruce and hemlock
and more cedars. The sun fell through on huckleberry bushes that had turned red with the autumn
frost. The hill flattened out and they were at the
edge of the muskeg, standing in the sunlight. Overhead a few white clouds drifted in a blue sky.

The moss of the muskeg was deep and thick and
spongy. It looked like old faded rose-and-gold bro-
cade that had been kept in a trunk for a hundred
years. Shallow ponds of dark water lay about in the
moss, and all around the edge, in the muskeg, dead
trees stood stark and white. Farther out the con-
torted trunks and branches of long-fallen cedars lay
like bleached bones on the wet moss. It was a place
where all was dying and decaying and no more life
would begin. On the far side the dark forest rose
again to climb another hill.

Jaimy said, "This must be it," and he crouched
down to look at the moss.

At first Florence couldn't see the cranberries. She
walked around bent over, peering at the ground, at
the strange old reds and dull golds of the moss, and
at the way the water bubbled up around her boots.
Then she saw the little berries and Jaimy discovered them too. They lay at the end of a hair-like
stem with their few leaves so deep in the moss that
they couldn't be seen. Jaimy walked boldly out
across the muskeg and found a place where there
were old branches and fallen trees. Here Ma could
sit while she picked. Even in the sunlight the place

had a secret, ghostly feeling about it that made them hurry. They all went to work picking as fast as they could. Jaimy took the far side and Florence worked along the side where they had come up.

She picked her way along the edge of the muskeg, feeling uneasy and watchful as though she were a trespasser. After a while she looked up and found that she was among the skeleton trees at the far end of the swamp and that the dark forest was just ahead of her. A feeling of panic set her heart pounding and she straightened and looked hastily around for Ma and Jaimy. She saw Ma picking her way among the dead stumps, and across on the far side Jaimy was working his way along the edge of one of the dark ponds. Coming toward her was Donny with his nose up, sniffing. The air had turned cold and the shadow of a cloud was traveling across the muskeg toward her, sliding over the moss, subduing its color. She felt a vague, inexplicable terror of this place and she had to make an effort for self-control when she bent down again to pick the little berries as she worked her way back to Ma.

Jaimy, with his gun slung over his shoulder, came from the far side to join them. "Let's eat," he said.

"Yes, let's," Ma agreed. "Here's a good log to sit on." She straightened up to rest her back. "I think we've got enough, don't you?" she asked, looking into the pails. "They're nearly a third full, and besides, this is such a queer place and I think it's getting cold."

Florence agreed quickly and brought the picnic basket to the log. "It is a queer place," she said, with a nervous laugh. "I feel as though someone were watching us."

Jaimy was about to speak when they heard a crashing in the brush across the muskeg. A doe dashed out of the forest, running and leaping through the ghost trees where Florence had been. In terror it raced through the dead trees, running for the beach, and close upon it came two huge timber wolves. Donny bristled and pointed, tail out and trembling. Jaimy raised his gun and shot. One wolf leapt in the air and fell and the other turned to streak off into the trees. Jaimy fired again and they could see the fur fly, but the second wolf kept on going and vanished into the forest. They could hear the tired deer dashing on toward the safety of the water.

"Mercy me, what a noise!" cried Ma, her hands over her ears.

Donny whined and watched Jaimy. It had all happened so quickly that Florence stood aghast, staring at the fallen wolf. Jaimy went toward it, cautiously, with Donny at his heels. Florence followed them over the spongy moss, fearful for Jaimy and with the terrified deer still vivid in her mind. Ma started to speak and then thought better of it. She stood up and replaced the sandwiches she had taken from the lunch basket. Then she waited, turning slowly around, peering into the shadowy forest on all sides of them.

The wolf lay on its side, tongue out, its black lips curled back from strong white fangs. It lay still, its huge feet spread as though frozen in a leap. Donny circled around it, sniffing suspiciously and refusing to come close.

"Man, what a beast!" Jaimy said, poking it cautiously with his rifle. "I'll bet he's seven feet if he's an inch."

Florence looked down at the wolf, at his fine furry ears and the thick pads on his feet and, suddenly, she was sorry that he was dead. "Why Jaimy," she said, "he's like a big dog except for his brush, like —like a prince of beasts."

"He may look like a pet to you," Jaimy answered, "but not to me!"

"But I thought he'd look horrible," she tried to explain. "You know—thin and scraggly and—mean. But Jaimy, look at him! He's a beautiful animal."

"He's killed enough deer to keep in fine shape. You'd be fatter yourself, if you ate a deer a week." He turned the wolf over carefully. "Man, he's heavy! But he's going to make a fine rug for beside my bed. I'm glad it's downhill to the skiff."

Together they dragged the wolf across the wet moss to where Ma stood. Ma said, "I think we should go. This is no place to picnic." She looked accusingly at the dead beast and started off across the muskeg, holding her skirts in one hand and the picnic basket in the other.

Jaimy laughed. "Hey, wait a minute! We're going with you."

That was the way with Jaimy. He seemed to be protected from intangible fears and suspicions. He seemed to be able to take his world without seeing the evil in it. With the wolf on his back he started after Ma's fleeing figure, laughing when he staggered under its weight. Hurrying, Florence dumped all their berries into one pail, filling it almost to overflowing. She left the other pails lying on the moss and, with Jaimy's heavy rifle over her shoulder, she took off after him like a routed soldier fleeing from an invisible enemy. Her gum boots sucked noisily in the wet moss as she tried to run, going between the twisted trees at the edge of the muskeg. Behind her the two lard pails shone brightly in the sun. Then a cloud mass moved in over the trees and its gray shadow crept slowly over the old rose and the dull gold of the muskeg and over the shining brown ponds and the stark trees until it was lost in the deep, whispering forest.

In the gloom of the big trees Florence stopped and looked wildly about her for Jaimy. Before her the dry brown moss of the forest floor, the dark tree trunks with their pale, hanging lichens seemed to end in impenetrable gloom. "Jaimy," she shrieked, suddenly terrified. "Jaimy!"

"For heaven's sake," Jaimy said, "what's the matter?"

There he was a short distance down the slope, resting his wolf on a windfall. Ma's voice came from somewhere beyond him. "We're right here, dear. Come along now. This is no place to loiter."

Ma showed great alacrity on the downgrade to the beach. She kept calling little encouraging words back to them and when Jaimy stopped to rest against a stump she said, "There, I can see the water through these wretched trees at last. We're almost out."

When they got out on the beach, Jaimy was breathless and wet with perspiration. When he pulled in the skiff his arms trembled, exhausted by the muscular tension of his effort, but he was excited and triumphant because he'd got his wolf out. Florence gazed across the open water to where the sun still shone on the opposite side of Klakas Inlet. Behind her the forest seemed full of lurking eyes and waiting danger. She put Jaimy's gun in the bow of the skiff and called to Donny to jump in. "Do let's hurry," she said. "We can eat the sandwiches on the way home."

Jaimy helped Ma into the skiff and she sat down on the stern seat with Donny beside her and the berries at her feet. Then they loaded the wolf into the bow and shoved off. Before she opened the sandwiches Ma cast one last hostile glance at the silent, formidable forest. "Such a place!" she said.

She adjusted her bonnet and smoothed her skirts and then she handed Jaimy a sandwich.

Florence rowed while Jaimy ate. The tide was ebbing and the rowing easy, but the vast wilderness about her was wild and lonely and she was conscious of the dead wolf in the bow behind her. She thought again of the doe, running for her life to the safety of the water. When they finally turned into the Narrows and rowed hard against the tide to get into the cove, she looked over her shoulder at the big white house and cried, "Oh, Ma! There's home!"

But they were no sooner in the cove than they knew something was wrong. Wails and cries such as they had never heard before poured forth from the Indian village and they could hear the dull rhythmic beat of drums. In front of Old Yelthnow's house women were crying shrill keening cries, rocking back and forth with arms and hands writhing. Clouds had covered the sky, shedding a gray light upon the cove, and the great Yelthnow house behind the women seemed melancholy and old as the ground on which it stood. The totem pole, the tallest in the village, stood inscrutable, its many figures rising one upon the other to the great carved wolf at the top, the symbol of Yelthnow's clan.

As Jaimy and Florence rowed in, the old medicine man, Quee-aunce, came forth from the low door of the house, wearing a fantastic headdress and a fringed blanket. He stopped and stared at the skiff. Then he strode through the wailing women, past the totem pole, and on to a group of old men standing on the beach. He spoke to them and pointed to the skiff with a bright, painted object he held in his hand. The old men turned and followed his look.

"What are they staring at?" Jaimy asked.

Ma said, "I don't know, but I think it's that wretched wolf."

The tide had fallen, leaving the shrunken cove with a wide band of beach all around it. As the skiff drew in below the Monroe house Gregory came running down from the store to meet the picnic party. At the same time the elders of the village, led by the old medicine man, came marching around the beach past the Indian houses, past the store, toward the place where the skiff would land.

Gregory, already there, grabbed the bow and pulled it up on the dark shale. "Heaven help us!" he exclaimed, looking at the dead wolf. "Old Yelth-now died—about two hours ago—and here you come in with a dead wolf." He helped Ma and Florence out. "Go on up to the house," he advised. "I'll meet this delegation."

The Indians were almost upon them but Ma held on to his arm. "Greg, what do they want?" she asked.

"I don't know," he answered, "but I'd guess old Quee-aunce is going to figure out that the shooting of this wolf had something to do with the chief's death. Go on now, hurry. This is no place for you."

He turned back to Jaimy. "Where did you get this?" he demanded.

But there was no time for Jaimy to answer. The old medicine man was there, looking fiercely at Gregory and pointing at the wolf and at Jaimy as he talked. His voice was ominous and it seemed to Florence that he was threatening Gregory. She hesitated, waiting.

Ma took her arm. "Come, dear," she said. "It sounds awful, I know, but you must remember that Greg can understand the words. It's really a terrible thing but we must let Gregory take care of it."

Reluctantly, Florence followed Ma to the house. She felt dazed and frightened and she kept looking back at Greg. But nothing changed. The old medicine man kept on talking in his threatening voice.

CHAPTER *10*

*M*A AND FLORENCE proceeded up the beach to the big house, not speaking until they were inside the door. To Florence it had never looked so welcoming; once inside they would be safe from the wild forest, from the wolves and from the Indians. They closed the door behind them, and the terrible wailing on the beach was diminished by the protecting walls. They could hear the sound of hammers over in the boathouse, real and reassuring, blotting out the strangeness of the day and establishing again the security of home. McDuff ran from the kitchen to meet them and stood in the dining-room door, blinking his round eyes and waving his fluffy tail slowly back and forth.

Ma went past him to the kitchen with her pail of
berries. "Oh, I'm so sorry," she said, "so sorry. Old
Yelthnow was a real friend to Pa." She put the pail
on the drainboard and automatically took the big
kettle to the pump and filled it.

Florence said, "You know, Ma, I had the oddest
feeling about that wolf all along." She put the
lunch basket on the table and opened the drafts in
the range. "Will they wail longer for Yelthnow because he was chief? It makes me nervous to hear
them."

"It's their way," Ma said. "They don't understand
the comfort of Our Lord. Poor Mrs. Yelthnow."

When the fire was going under the kettle they
went upstairs to change their clothes. In the front
of the house the wailing was louder again and Ma
sighed. "I'm going to have forty winks, dear; then
we'll have tea. Try to rest for a few minutes—it's
been such a queer day."

But Florence could not rest nor did she feel
weary. She looked down at the beach through the
lace curtains of her bedroom window, removing her
long hatpin as she watched Gregory and Jaimy
where they stood facing the old medicine man and
his followers. The tide had fallen and now the bow
of the skiff rested on the shale. The wolf lay in it
with his head and one paw on the gunwale, looking
almost alive. In the stern she could see Ma's umbrella and the blanket where they had left them.
Across the cove the old Yelthnow house looked

gloomy and dark and the women in front of it rocked and wailed. From the top of the tall totem pole the great wolf looked down with huge staring eyes.

Gregory's eyes never left the face of the medicine man. He looked young, standing there, and stern; Florence had never seen him look so stern before. Behind him, Jaimy's face was solemn and puzzled as he watched. Drawing a chair up to the window, Florence sat down and removed her short gum boots, feeling herself growing tense and nervous but knowing that the wailing would not stop—would not stop for days. She took off her old dress and hung it over the foot of her bed so the wet hem could dry. The old medicine man talked on and on, pointing to Jaimy's wolf and to the forest and to the Yelthnow totem pole. Then suddenly he stopped and stood looking at Greg. Without a pause Gregory Monroe began talking. He talked on and on as old Quee-aunce had done, and he pointed to the store, the house, and the sky.

Florence poured water from the big jug into the basin and washed hastily, feeling her skin tingle in the chill of the room. She was buttoning the bodice of her green twill when she saw the old medicine man turn away from the skiff and march back to the village. The old men of the tribe followed him, some of them talking, others shaking their heads in silence. Below the window Jaimy and Greg lugged the wolf around the corner of the house to the shed.

Florence hurried downstairs to rescue Ma's umbrella and to get something ready for tea.

It was almost five o'clock when Ma came down.
Florence had the fire in the sitting room burning
brightly and the door of the stove open so that the
light made shadows dance in the dusky room. Outside, the clouds hung low in a world of gray light
and no wind stirred the still water of the cove. The
tide, rising again, flowed smoothly in through the
islands and the gulls circled high before winging
out to the west. Three old women with shawls over
their heads walked out to the point beyond the last
house in the village and squatted on the rocks,
where they began wailing and rocking, each in
turn so that no moment passed in silence. Behind
their cries, like the distant sound of the sea, came
the prolonged doleful chanting inside the great
Yelthnow house.

Jaimy and Greg had skinned the wolf and buried
its carcass at the back of the garden; the stretched
hide they hid behind the woodpile in the shed.
They sat now around the stove, reluctant to light
the lamps so early, as Greg tried to explain to them
what he thought the medicine man meant to do.

"You've got to realize that this is serious," he
began, looking at Alec. He sat across the table from
Ma with his cup steaming before him and the firelight brightening one side of his face. Alec, in Pa's
chair, leaned back comfortably, chewing a biscuit.
On the other side of the open stove, Florence sat in

the shadow with the firelight shining on her knees and on her face when she leaned forward to sip her tea. The keening on the point went on without pause.

"It's a sad thing the old chief died," Alec said. "Pa will be sorry. But I can't see it's anything for us to get excited about."

Greg went on trying to explain but his voice was losing its patience. "I'm trying to tell you that Quee-aunce will seize upon anything, anything he can, to get the young men on his side. He'll try to scare them. He'll revive all the old superstitions and try to make them believe that when Jaimy killed the wolf, he killed Old Yelthnow."

Jaimy, sitting near Florence, had had his chair tipped back and now he let it down with a thump. "Great Scott, Greg!" he cried. "How can he figure that out?"

"He couldn't have hoped for a better opportunity," Greg said. "He has hated the Yelthnow clan for years because Yelthnow made an agreement with Pa. Now, by conniving with Young Paul, he hopes to have a chief whom he can influence. He hates the whites and he knows that Pa's store does more toward the progress of the people than even the mission at Howkan. And the more progress the Indians make, the less power will he have over them."

"Why, Greg," Ma said. "You mustn't talk so!"

Alec recrossed his long legs. "It is their custom,"

he said, "to howl over their dead. If you take my
advice, Greg, you'll keep out of their plots and their
heathen practices. I see no reason why we should
concern ourselves." He sat with his red hair and
beard catching the firelight, looking as Pa might
have looked as a young man.

"You'd concern yourself quick enough if they decided to take a shot at Jaimy or to burn the store,"
Greg said hotly. "I tell you this business of the wolf
is all they needed to build up a chance for Young
Paul and Quee-aunce to oust Konutkan."

Florence turned to her brother, feeling for the
first time that he was exaggerating the danger.
"Oh, Greg," she cried, "they wouldn't do that! Why,
Greg, what do you mean?" In the pause that followed her anxious question the chanting and wailing in the village seemed to carry a warning of
danger.

Alec said, "Gregory, hold your tongue. If Pa
were here he'd have none of this. You've no right
to frighten Ma and Florence." Alec had the Scots-
man's belief in the rightness of his own thinking and
he rejected anything that he himself could not understand.

Gregory's face flushed and he got up and walked
to the front of the room and back. When he spoke
it was not to Alec but to Ma and Florence. "If Pa
were here," he said, "at least he'd know what's going on." With an impatient shake of his dark head
and a growing despair in his voice he went on.

"Can't you see what old Quee-aunce is doing? This is the first time in two years he's had a chance to turn his people back to the old ways. Do you think *he* wants them to learn *our* ways?" He turned with a hopeless gesture to his brother. "Great Scott, Alec, you know that if Pa's store and the Reverend's mission last long enough there won't *be* any more medicine men—and so does he. He can influence the old people and he'll try to control the young ones. Who can blame him? If he can convince them that Old Yelthnow died because Jaimy shot a wolf in a forbidden place, he'll do it and Young Paul will support him. And, mark you, if this village turns against us, all of Pa's work will have been for nothing."

Alec said, "Nonsense. It's no affair of ours. And what do you propose to do, anyway? You must be daft to think they'd harm Jaimy." He got to his feet and put his cup on the tea tray. "It's going to be a cold night," he said, sniffing as though he could smell the outside air. "Come, Jaimy, we'll fill the wood boxes."

Bewildered and embarrassed, Jaimy got up. "That confounded beast!" he exclaimed. "Is there anything I can do about it, Greg?"

Ma put her hand on Jaimy's arm as he passed her chair. "It wasn't your fault, dear. That wretched beast had no business chasing that poor little doe. And I'm sure poor Mrs. Yelthnow will not confuse her late husband with a wolf."

Greg said: "Wait a minute, Alec. I'm trying to tell you that there are some things we *can* do. You know Pa always sends something over to the village when anyone dies. The Yelthnows should have something extra. I thought I'd take half a dozen blankets over to their house tomorrow."

"Three's enough," said Alec. "It's a mistake to be overlavish."

Greg sighed and sat down again, passing his cup to Ma. "We've got to support Konutkan," he said wearily. "Konutkan and his brothers and a few others will see what Quee-aunce and Paul are trying to do."

"We've got to mind our own business," said Alec, already in the hall on his way to replenish the wood box.

That night there was a fire on the beach and all night long the old women wailed. Under the hovering rainless clouds no wind blew. The flat dark water of the cove reflected the flickering firelight and the great eyes on the totem poles came in and out of the wavering shadows, huge and alive. In her big room Florence lay with the comforter pulled up to her chin, sleepless and disturbed by the wavering light on the wide windows. The bed had been cold when she got in and her feet were still tucked up under the folds of her long gown. She felt lonely and scared but she was ashamed to go into Ma's room and confess it. She missed Laura because, somehow, it was easier to be brave when her little sister was there. She tried to think of Beldon and of her wedding but the wild keening in the village broke into her thoughts and she pulled her pillow over her head to try to keep it out. It went on all night and she did not sleep until the gray dawn had diminished the light of the fire. Then the keening stopped and only the monotonous chanting could be heard.

When Gregory took the blankets to the Yelthnow house Ma put on her bonnet and went with him, taking one of her own shawls to give to Mrs. Yelthnow. "Poor thing," Ma said. "There is so little we can do to comfort her." When they came back Greg told how they were met with hostile looks and silence and that Ma had gone to the old chief's wife where she sat weeping and had put the shawl around her shoulders and prayed to God to comfort her.

"The poor thing," Ma said, "weeping in that big dark house with those awful totems staring down at her."

At the end of two more days even Alec showed the strain of sleeplessness. Greg went each morning to the store, hoping that some of the people would come and talk to him. But none came, not even Nakatla. The old Indian men and women who had been friendly before now kept their faces averted from the Monroe house and none set foot on the walk to the store. Einar Gren suggested to Alec that he come and stay in the house because no

one could tell what might happen when the young
men came back to the village from Howkan. When
Alec spoke to Ma about it, she went right out to the
kitchen where Einar was waiting.

"Do bring your things right in, Mr. Gren," she
urged. "You are most welcome. We have wanted
you right along."

She sent Florence to air the spare room and see
that there were matches in the box and oil in the
lamp. Einar moved in, shy and apologetic, with his
duffel bag full of clean shirts and socks, and his
Winchester rifle and his Lutheran Bible. Every
morning he made his own bed and he wouldn't
wash in his basin but instead used the granite one
in the shed and kept his towel there even in the increasing cold. With his presence in the house Florence's fear subsided. He was Beldon Craig's man
and with him there seemed to come Beldon's protection.

The next morning the clouds were high and a
cold wind came in puffs out of the north, wrinkling
the steely water and sending the fog out to sea.
From the upstairs window Florence could look
through the Narrows far out over Cordova Bay.
The trees of the islands stood dark and wintry
against the gray sky, and the leaves of the crab
apple fell fluttering to the beach with every puff of
wind. The day was dark but so clear was the air
that the long line of Cape Muzon could be seen on
the south horizon, far, far away. During the morn-

ing as she tidied up the bedrooms Florence paused often to look out through the Narrows, and she was the first to see the Indian canoes returning from Howkan.

They must have camped all night on Sukkwan because they came out from behind the islands to the north, and when she saw them they were already quite near the Narrows. With a cry of excitement she ran downstairs to tell Ma. She kept on running through the kitchen and over to the boathouse to tell the boys and Einar. Jaimy came out to watch the canoes come in but Alec kept on working.

"You're excited, Flossie," he reproved her. "Run back to the house now and tend to your own trifles. They always carry on when any of them dies."

"But, Alec," she began, "Greg says . . ."

"Greg is full of nonsense, Indian nonsense!" Alec said, caustically. "Their goings on are no business of ours, I tell you."

Einar Gren stopped his work and looked at them. "Do not worry, Miss Monroe," he said. "We keep our eyes and ears open."

Alec's crossness and Einar's calm were reassuring in themselves, but the canoes were in the Narrows now and the chanting of the paddlers drifted into the cove. She couldn't quell her fear for Jaimy. "Do come and stay in the house," she begged, plucking at his sleeve. "Oh, please do."

He jerked away and turned back to the boathouse. "Don't be a ninny," he said. "Do you think I'm going to run and hide like a rabbit?"

Discouraged and full of apprehension, Florence returned to the house. "I'm going to watch from the window upstairs," she told Ma. "I'm so worried about Jaimy. Oh, Ma, I do think he ought to be careful."

Ma said, "Don't fret about it, dear. I'm relieved that they've come. Surely they'll get the funeral over within a day or two and that awful wailing will stop."

Florence went to watch in Ma's room because it had, besides the front windows overlooking the cove, a side window from which she could see the store. When she got there the canoe bringing the young men of Klinkwan back again was just coming into the cove. The women and old men of the village were gathered on the beach and the crying and wailing rose and fell in wave after wave of disconsolate sound. Three great war canoes from Howkan with high overhanging prows and sterns came in single file through the narrow entrance to the cove. They were coming to bury Old Yelthnow and they would be paid with blankets and feasting as was the custom of the people. The huge dugouts, as long as the *Laura M.*, filled the cove. The paddlers and the women sitting among them chanted and moaned as they drew up to the beach beneath the tall totem poles of Klinkwan.

As the prows touched the dark shale old Quee-

aunce appeared in the door of the Yelthnow house.
Impressive in his ceremonial regalia, he stood like
a high priest surveying the scene before him. Then
he walked down the path to the beach and there
was a sudden silence as he began to harangue the
people. He stood facing the canoes, whose prows
just touched the shore, the men holding them there
with the paddles. As he talked, Young Paul came
close to him, and the other Yelthnow nephews and
young men of Klinkwan drew nearer. Florence
could see their intent faces as they watched him
and listened. He talked on and on, standing in the
clear cold light, his voice rising and falling but
never stopping. An hour passed and he still talked,
and Florence could see that the people were getting
excited. At intervals their silence was broken by
cries and moans. When Quee-aunce finally stopped
they climbed out of the canoes, crying and wailing
and shouting. Young Paul began talking and they
stopped to listen. Talking vehemently, he gestic-
ulated in the direction of the Monroe house. To her
horror Florence saw the medicine man and the dead
chief's nephew break away from the crowd and
come walking along the beach toward the house.
Their dark faces were surly and they walked fast
and close together.

Then she saw Gregory start down the beach to
meet them. He came out of the store and waded
through the tall beach grass. He was hatless and
puffs of wind stirred his hair as he walked a little

way toward the village. He stopped, just below the store—Pa's dividing line—and waited there for Quee-aunce and Young Paul. He stood with his arms folded and his feet apart. He did not speak, but waited for the medicine man to begin.

*A*T THE dinner table Gregory told them what had taken place on the beach. Anxious and distraught, he ate little and overemphasized his words in his effort to make them understand that there was real danger. Florence thought the painful scene would never come to an end. Alec was behaving just like Pa, telling Greg to leave the Indians alone—not to listen to their threats—but Florence couldn't help feeling that if Pa were there he'd see it Greg's way.

"But don't you see?" Greg argued. "Quee-aunce and Young Paul together would reject every iota of Pa's civilizing influence, including the store, if

they thought they could gain control over the
people. These Indians have just begun to learn
civilized ways. They still fear the animal spirits,
and the medicine man will take advantage of that.
He'll try to swing them back to the old superstitions. It's up to us to support Konutkan. If Young
Paul ousts him, there'll be no more progress in this
village. Konutkan is the rightful chief and we must
stand by him."

Greg paused and looked at them all as though
hoping for some support. "That delegation came
over here this morning to demand that I give them
Jaimy's wolf," he went on. "You know what that
means. The old medicine man is clever enough to
persuade them that we killed their chief when Jaimy
shot that wolf. We must prove to them that he's
a faker and that he and Paul are working together
to fool them."

"Your meddling will only make matters worse,"
Alec said. "Let them choose their own chief—how-
ever they want to. It will do you well to remember,
Greg, what Pa said to you before he went south.
You mind your business and they'll mind theirs."

"All right." Gregory spoke in a resigned voice
and got up to leave the table. "But let me tell you
this. If Young Paul and Quee-aunce succeed in
ousting Konutkan and turning the people against
us, there will be no room in this country for the
Monroe family, or for the mission at Howkan,
either."

Gregory started out of the room and then he stopped, seeing Ma's troubled face. "I don't mean to go against Pa," he said. "If Pa were here he'd see that *something* ought to be done." He went out then, pale and deeply troubled.

"They'll bury their old chief and get it all settled," Alec said, looking uncomfortable. "It's bad of Greg to worry you with all this."

"Gregory may be mistaken," Ma said, "but he means to do right. That's all any of us can do, Alec."

They finished the meal in silence and Florence was glad she had the work of clearing away afterwards. In the afternoon she and Ma opened the sewing machine for the first time. They had enough blue flannel legs basted together now to begin on the stitching. It took them all afternoon learning to thread the machine, because they kept looking out of the windows hoping to see the big canoes taking Old Yelthnow's body over to the burial point. But not once during the day did anyone appear on the beach. The thud of the drums and the strange chanting went on and on. It was not until late afternoon that the people began to come out of their houses, walk to the great Yelthnow house, and enter the low door.

As the day grew darker, shadows gathered in the corners of the Monroe dining room. Ma stood up with a sigh, putting the instruction book back in a drawer of the sewing machine. "Oh my, Florence," she said, "sometimes it's hard to cope with things!"

"It's that chanting!" Florence said. "And Greg
and Alec quarreling." Her own nerves were on
edge. She got up and closed the machine. "I'll put
the kettle on," she said. "It's time for tea, anyway."

When tea was ready, Florence stepped out on
the back porch as was her custom and called to the
boys, who were working in the boathouse. Jaimy
came out first, as usual, and started for the house.
He was barely on his way when a shot was fired
from the woods. As he ducked his head with a
quick involuntary movement, Florence screamed
and Einar Gren, making a dive out of the boathouse, dragged Jaimy down off the walk to the
ground. Alec yelled, "Get inside, Flossie!" He came
boldly out on the walk and faced the woods. "Come
out of there!" he demanded.

Greg ran from the store to the house and they
all stood there for a moment and stared at Jaimy,
still pinned to the ground by Einar's strong hand.

Alec, getting no reply from the woods, went into
the house and came back with his rifle. He stalked
about in the woods back of the house in such a rage
that Ma and Florence hoped he would find no one.
When he came back, still angry and balked by his
fruitless search, he turned unreasonably on Greg.
"This comes from your meddling!" he shouted. "If
you'd leave those savages alone, they'd leave us
alone. You'll keep on about this wolf until you get
Jaimy killed."

Jaimy, shaken and bewildered, tried to point out to Alec that Greg had merely warned them, but Alec persisted in his stubborn belief that if Gregory had ignored the Indians nothing would have happened.

It was Ma who restored peace. "We must all do right as God gives us to see the right," she said. "Let us have peace in our own house if we expect peace from others."

In the evening they all went to the sitting room with Einar Gren added to their number, to listen to Alec read out of the Bible. He chose the Acts of the Apostles and read of Paul's journey through Greece. They all sat around the stove and the big room was full of shadows. Alec sat in Pa's chair with a lamp at his elbow. There was another lamp on the round cherry-wood table and Greg sat just outside its rim of light. The others all faced the stove and the firelight from its open doors shone on their faces. All were quiet and solemn as they listended to Alec. Ma's darning lay unheeded on the table. While Alec was reading, the drums in the village stopped and Florence found herself waiting for them to begin again, because somehow their silence seemed more ominous than their rhythmic beat. Alec kept right on reading and she could not tell whether he noticed or not, but Gregory stirred in his chair and she knew that he was listening. A few minutes later there was a knock at the kitchen

door. Gregory sprang to his feet and started out of
the room with Donny at his heels.

Florence felt the blood drain from her face. She
got up and looked at the others. She could see that
they had not heard the knock. "There's someone at
the door," she said, "the kitchen door," and walked
out of the room. But Gregory had already vanished
into the darkness of the dining room. She was in
the hall when the knock came again and she heard
the stir in the room behind her. She heard her
name called but she kept on after Gregory. She
wanted to run but she could only walk, compelled
as though in a nightmare toward something she
dreaded. In the darkness she bumped against the
dining-room table. "Greg!" she called in a whisper.
"Greg, come back." She felt a cold draft on her feet
and knew that Greg had opened the door without
waiting to light the lamp.

Then Alec came into the room from the hall,
holding a lamp above his head. Her long shadow
jumped into the kitchen before her and she could
see Gregory there with the door wide open. He
turned and said sharply, "Keep that light out of the
kitchen!" Then he spoke rapidly in Haida and stood
back from the door.

Florence stopped in her tracks just within the
kitchen as Nakatla stepped in out of the darkness.
She wore no headkerchief and no shawl, only a cot-
ton waist and a long purple skirt. Her hair hung
in two long braids, making her look young, almost

childlike, as she stood with her back to the door, twisting her small brown hands together and regarding the Monroes with wide, doubtful eyes.

For a moment no one spoke. Then Alec put the lamp on the table in the dining room and all the shadows leapt upward, Florence's own shadow rising like a shield above Nakatla. The Indian girl turned to Gregory and spoke urgently in her own language, the softly accented words flowing smoothly on in her low voice.

Alec came forward. "What is this, Gregory?" he asked. "What does this girl want?"

Gregory faced them there in the semidarkness with just a dull reflection of lamplight on his face. "There's no time to argue," he said. "Nakatla says the Quee-aunce has got the village worked up to a point where they'll do violence to get hold of that confounded wolf. And if they get it, he'll use it to scare the people into thinking Jaimy was really the cause of Yelthnow's death. Then he'll demand indemnities . . ." Greg stopped and looked at them earnestly. "We can't let this happen. I'm going to the village now and make them listen to Konutkan and to me." He looked directly at Alec. "You can come if you want to," he said.

Alec stepped close to Greg. "Have you lost your head completely?" he said. "Send this girl back. Tell her we'll talk to them at the store in the morning."

Greg returned his gaze and the brothers stood

there, the dark one and the red one, like enemies
staring at each other.

Gregory said: "Nakatla has taken her life in her
hands to come over here and warn us. Do you
think she would do that for nothing? The people
will listen to me and I may be able to swing them
back to reason. I want to get over there before he
works them up to a hysterical pitch." He walked
away from Alec and opened the door. Nakatla
went silently out and he followed her.

Ma ran to the door and held it open. "I'll be
back," Greg said, and they heard his footsteps on
the walk as he went past the windows in the dark.

At midnight Ma was dozing in her chair. They
had all stopped talking and Alec had stopped
tramping around the house like a night watchman.
Jaimy sat at the window of the dark room, staring
through the night in the direction of the village. In
the kitchen Einar Gren waited so quietly that Florence feared from time to time that he had fallen
asleep. He had taken up his watch there right after
Greg had gone. Ma had insisted that they put out
the lamps and she had prayed to the Good Shep-
herd to give Gregory the right words to make peace
in the village and to bring him back safely. But
Greg had been gone for three hours now. Florence
had passed the point of sleepiness and she sat
rigidly in her chair, suffering in her anxiety for her
brother's safety. She knew that it was the custom

of the Indians to talk for hours when anything of importance came up; the greatest talker often won the day. Greg would have to talk for hours too, if he was to impress them.

To cheer the family, as well as himself, Jaimy said: "There'd be a hullabaloo if they were fighting. As long as they're quiet it's all right, old Greg's getting somewhere." But he sat on nervously at the window, a darker bulk against the darkness.

For a long time Ma sat rocking with McDuff in her lap. Then she stopped rocking and it grew very quiet. Only the wailing of the old women on the point went on and on. But when the big clock in the hall struck twelve, Alec jumped to his feet noisily, bumping the table at his side with a sudden movement that startled them all.

"By Heaven," he shouted, "we'll get our rifles and go over there. Gregory must have gone off his head."

Ma stirred in her chair and Florence could hear the catch in her breath. "That is not the way, Alec," she said. "Gregory has chosen to do this. None of us supported him. It is not for us to interfere."

Her voice was firm but it was so sad and forlorn that Florence was drawn through the darkness to her side. She knelt on the floor beside the rocking chair and buried her face in Ma's lap. "Oh dear," she cried, "oh dear. What can we do?" She wept into McDuff's fur and Donny came over and thrust his nose under her arm, whining.

Ma stroked her head and murmured, "There, dear, you're overtired. It'll all work out in God's good time. It'll all work out."

Jaimy shifted on his chair at the window. "Hey, Sis," he said, "don't do that. Old Greg'll make it all right. You wait and see." But his voice nearly broke and she heard him sniffle as he turned back to the window. She could hear McDuff purring loudly under her ear and she dabbed her nose with her handkerchief.

"Crying does no good, Flossie," Alec said gruffly. He came and stood near Ma's chair. "We'll just have to wait. Should I make you some tea?"

"Oh Alec, do," Ma said. "We're all overstrained. It'll do us good. And Alec," she went on as he made his way to the door in the dark, "do ask poor Mr. Gren to come in. He's been watching in the kitchen for hours."

Florence sighed and got to her feet, relieved that they were all talking again. She kissed Ma. "You're so comforting," she said tremulously.

"Couldn't we light a candle?" Jaimy asked.

"Yes, Jaimy," Ma said immediately, "light the lamps, dear. Greg should know that we're waiting for him—that we trust him."

"I'll light one lamp," Jaimy said, "and I'll take a candle to Alec."

"Yes, Jaimy, do. Oh, it's a mistake to doubt," Ma added as though to herself.

It was going on toward one o'clock before Gregory came back. They had brought the tea to the sitting room and persuaded Einar Gren to join them. "I think your boy knows them," he said to Ma. "He will show them their mistake."

They were sitting with their tea and bread and butter when they heard the kitchen door open and close. Before anyone could move Ma called, "Is that you, Gregory?"

"Yes, Ma," he answered. "It took a lot of talking but it's settled now."

Jaimy jumped up and grabbed the lamp. He was in the hall in a few strides. "Hey, Greg, wait. Here's a light!" he shouted.

Florence followed him and they met Gregory coming through the dining room. "Oh, Greg!" Florence cried. She clung to his arm, so thankful he was back that she forgot why he had gone. "Oh, Greg," she cried again, "you smell smoky"—she was laughing now—"the way I did after my night over there."

"I'm glad you stayed up," Greg said. "If you hadn't I'd have wakened you. You should have seen it!" His face was pale and his gray eyes dark and shining with excitement. When he walked into the sitting room and spoke, his voice was intense and stirring. "We won the night," he said to them all. "You should have heard Mrs. Yelthnow. She was magnificent. You should have heard her!"

Ma said, "Sit down, Gregory, and tell us about

it." She removed the cozy from the teapot and poured a cup of tea for Greg.

He pulled a footstool near her chair and sat down, taking the tea she offered. Jaimy put the lamp on the table and squatted down on his heels beside Gregory. "How did you do it, old fellow?" he asked, his voice full of admiration. "How in thunder did you do it?"

Gregory was drinking his tea and Florence could see his hands shake ever so slightly. She pulled her chair around so she could face him, "I'm so glad you're home," she said, leaning forward and looking at him. "You're tired. You must be tired out. Jaimy, let him wait until morning. He'll tell us about it in the morning."

"No," Gregory said, "I'll tell you now. I'm not sleepy." He handed his cup to Ma for more tea. Then he grinned at Jaimy. "I talked," he said. "Konutkan and I outtalked Young Paul and Quee-aunce."

"Did they tell you who fired that shot at Jaimy?" Alec asked.

"I didn't ask them," Greg said. "But you can depend upon it Konutkan will not let it go. If he can't find the culprit he'll pay indemnities himself. These people always make amends where amends are due—when they understand." He drank his tea and looked up at Ma. "I haven't told you the best of it yet," he began.

"If you didn't talk to them about that," said Alec,

"what on earth did you talk about? They'll pay a few trinkets for Jaimy's life, I suppose?"

"I'm not dead," Jaimy said impatiently. "Let Greg tell about it!"

Greg looked at Alec. "I knew that if we could beat this move of Quee-aunce's everything else would be all right," he explained patiently. "That was the important thing tonight. The rest can be worked out, because Konutkan is progressive and he'll carry on as Old Yelthnow did." He paused, and suddenly the excitement that had buoyed him up was gone. He looked very tired.

Ma reached out and stroked his head. "What was the 'best' thing you were going to tell me?" she asked.

"I wanted to tell you about Mrs. Yelthnow," Greg continued, reviving. "We couldn't have won without her. She stood up there and told them all how Old Yelthnow felt about Pa. She said that he had asked to be buried on Our Point to show his fellowship with Mr. Monroe. She went on to say that Jaimy had killed a wolf in a forbidden place and that now its spirit was with the Monroes, and the Monroes and the Yelthnows were brothers, and also"—here Greg smiled at Ma—"and also that the God of Mrs. Monroe would help the Yelthnow house because Mrs. Monroe had asked Him to."

"It's an answer to our prayer," Ma said.

"She was amazing," Greg went on. "I talked myself hoarse trying to show why Young Paul was in-

fluencing the young men to follow Quee-aunce.
When she saw that Paul actually had the audacity
to aspire to the old chief's place she stood up and
lit into them all. Man, oh, man, she had them hanging their heads and one by one the young men
moved away from Quee-aunce until he sat there
with only the old men around him and not all of
them. Young Paul's political life is over."

"Young Paul ought to be run off the beach," Alec
declared, getting to his feet. "But we needn't sit
here all night talking about it." He started off to
bed, calling back from the hall, "Come, Greg, you're
tiring Ma."

Ma got up, letting McDuff slide down her skirt
to the floor. "It's only because Alec's so concerned
for you that he's so cross, Gregory," she said. "You
must go to bed yourself. You've earned your rest."
She kissed Greg and patted his head. "I'm proud of
you, dear."

Jaimy brought a candle from the rack in the hall
and lit it for her. They could hear her rustling skirts
on the stairs. Jaimy followed her, telling Greg that
he would light the lamp in his room. Einar got up
with a quiet good night and they heard the stairs
creak under his weight. Greg dropped his head in
his hands and sat there silent, in an attitude of utter
weariness.

"Greg," Florence said softly. "Greg, is there anything the matter?"

For a moment longer he sat there and then he

got to his feet and held out his hands. She took them and let him pull her to her feet. "No, there's nothing the matter—not really the matter," he said.

They lit their candles and blew out the lamp. Greg closed the drafts in the stove. He followed a little behind her on the stairs. "When you're an old lady with white hair and spectacles, you'll remember this night, won't you?" he said.

"Why, Greg, of course I'll remember." She spoke low in case Alec had already got to sleep. "Why did you say that?"

At the head of the stairs they stopped and whispered. "When you tell Bel about this," he said, ignoring her question, "remember, I respect the Indians. Always remember that."

"Greg, there *is* something the matter," she whispered, suddenly filled with instinctive alarm. "What is it?"

"It's the hour of the night and those poor old women crying on the point for Old Yelthnow," he said. He grinned his crooked grin and held up his candle and looked at her. "It's the tears and the grief that never need to be!" Then he turned suddenly away, saying good night, and walked to the door of his room.

She watched him go in and close the door. He did not look back. She went along the hall to her own room at the front of the house, uneasy and tired, too sleepy to labor over Greg's meaning. Greg was always so hard to understand.

CHAPTER 12

WHEN Florence woke in the morning it was to find Ma standing in her door. "Come, dear, wake up! It's shocking late. The boys are already at work." Ma opened the door wide to let in the heat from the hall. "There's a fire in my room," she added. "Get your clothes and dress in there."

"Yes, Ma," Florence said sleepily.

"Don't go to sleep again," Ma warned. "Oh my, it's nice to get up and know that peace is restored again!"

Florence roused herself and swung her long legs out of bed. She groped around with her feet to find her bedroom slippers. "Yes, Ma," she said again, "I'll hurry."

With the goose flesh crawling up her back she flew around the cold room gathering her clothes for the dash to Ma's stove. She dressed quickly, thinking of Greg. She wanted to talk to Greg. Looking in the glass as she made curls of her front hair, she met her own eyes and frowned thoughtfully. It *was* nice to wake up and know that peace was restored; but Greg knew that last night, she told herself, and he had not been happy. With a last touch to her curls she ran into the hall and down the stairs.

In the lower hall she met old Mary on her way to the sitting room with a broom and dustpan. "Oh, Mary," she cried, "you're back! Good morning!"

"Mary knows," the old slave woman answered, going across the hall and into the sitting room.

The cryptic answer brought Florence a brief flash of warning, but so intent was she on finding her brother that she let it go unheeded. She ran on through the dining room to the kitchen. In the doorway she was stopped short by the sight of Ma's face, as she stood beside the table, holding a letter in one hand and the key to the store in the other.

Her eyes were on the letter and her face was as white as the paper; it looked pinched and shrunken as though she had suddenly grown thin. Her lips were moving and Florence could see that she was saying Gregory's name over and over again, soundlessly. Shocked and frightened, Florence walked across the kitchen. "Ma," she whispered, "Ma, what is it?"

But Ma did not reply, did not even seem to see
her. She dropped the letter and the key on the
table and the key made a little rattle. As she walked
out of the kitchen she looked at Florence but she
seemed to be looking past her. She went upstairs
and Florance heard the door of her room close.
Left standing there in the kitchen, with the kettle
singing on the range, Florence was more frightened
than she had ever been before. Not the sea or the
wilderness, not the Indians or the loneliness had
ever frightened her like this. Trembling, she went
to the table and picked up the letter and read it.
Gregory wrote in a flying sort of script that was
difficult to read. She sat down and bent over the
letter, her brows drawn together in the effort to
read fast.

Dear Ma:
    May God forgive me for the pain I am causing
you. It is better for me to go away than to stay
here and bring what I know will seem only disgrace
to Pa in our own house. There is no way to say this
except to say it outright and pray that you will
understand. I have gone away with Nakatla and
we shall be married in Wrangell. Because of her
love for me she risked her life to warn us last night.
She has been coming to the store every day for
months to talk to me or just to look at me and I
have grown very fond of her. Since last night there
will be many in the village who will be her enemies.
I must protect her.

Oh, Ma, believe me, I am not doing this lightly. I see no other honorable way. I know that Pa will never forgive me. There is no understanding between him and me. To him I will be a squaw man and a disgrace. But it is no disgrace to marry Nakatla. I have no misgivings about that. The dreadful thing is the pain I am bringing to you. Forgive me if you can and remember always that I love you.

Your son,
Gregory

Unable to believe the words, Florence sat reading them again and again. She picked up the key to the store and looked at it, remembering that long ago she had foreseen that Gregory would come to some hurt in this country. But she had never really faced the thought that this might happen. Gregory, her own brother, Gregory was a—she could hardly bring herself to think the dreadful word. Oh, he was not, he couldn't be a squaw man. Alec would stop him. She would run and get Alec.

She went to the door and opened it, and stood there, feeling the cold air on her face. "It's the grief and pain that need not be!" That's what Gregory had said last night, standing at the head of the stairs with the candlelight in his eyes. She looked down at the smooth white paper, warm now in her hands, and she stepped back and closed the door. Tears streamed down her face and, crying uncontrollably, she ran for the stairs and Ma's room.

Ma's door was closed and she hesitated, feeling
the rebuff of the blank panels. For the first time in
her life she realized that it was no longer her right
to give way to tears in the comfort of Ma's lap. She
looked down at the letter in her hand, at the words,
"Your son," and she knew that Ma's grief was beyond her own. Softly she tapped on the door; then
she opened it. Ma was sitting in her low rocker
beside the cold stove, rocking back and forth, weeping into her white handkerchief.

Florence had never before seen her mother cry.
She stood now, her own tears stopped, and her heart
pounding painfully. Ma had withstood so much.
In the loneliness and anxiety of their life in this new
country, it had always been Ma whose faith and
courage had sustained them. It was shocking to see
Ma break down, Ma whose tranquility had seemed
invulnerable. Uneasily, she walked across the room
to her chair. But when she got there, Ma's desolation was like a gulf between them and she did not
know what to say. She put the key on the writing
desk and looked again at the letter in her hand.
How could Ma ever face it, face telling Pa that his
son had gone away with an Indian girl? She put
the letter in Ma's lap and stood looking down at her
as she sat rocking back and forth with her face
in her hands. Ma would never see Gregory again.

Too stricken and fearful to speak, Florence shook
down the gray ashes in the stove and built a new
fire. She felt that their world had collapsed on their

heads. But somewhere within her Pa's hard disci-
pline kept her steady. She drew the armchair before the fire and put the footstool in front of it, her
throat aching with her effort not to cry.

"Do sit here where it's warm," she pleaded. "Let
me put your shawl around you." Yearning to comfort Ma, she talked on. "Gregory loves you, I know
he does. It's just that he couldn't stand it here."
Her own love for her brother made her continue.
"He hated it so—at first. And then he got so he
didn't care what happened to his life."

Desolate and wordless, Ma moved to the armchair
and sat there staring ahead of her at nothing.

"I'll bring you a cup of hot tea," Florence said
anxiously. She hurried from the room, closing the
door softly as one would the door of a sick room.
She had known grief and loneliness and danger in
this wild country but always there had been the
solidarity of the Monroes behind her, and always
there had been Ma to comfort her. But now the
family life was broken. As she made the tea she
was overcome with despair and she began to cry
again. Then she thought of Ma up there in her
room with Greg's letter and she thought that Ma
might die; it might be more than she could bear.
She put the cups on the tray and hurried back upstairs. Fearfully, she tapped on the door.

"Come in, dear," Ma said.

At the sound of her voice Florence entered the

room, almost overcome with gratitude and love.
"Ma, are you all right?"

"Yes, dear." She sat in the armchair looking
peaked and small but her voice was steady now.
"Don't be distressed, dear," she went on. "Gregory
made his decision with honorable intention. We
must remember that it was difficult, very difficult
for him." Ma looked so sad that Florence thought
her heart would break.

She poured the tea and sat down on the footstool.
"Shall I tell the boys?" she asked, wishing to spare
Ma. "Shall I tell Alec?"

Ma sipped her tea. "No, dear," she said, "I must
tell Alec myself. I am quite restored now. You
mustn't worry about me. God works wonders in
devious ways that are hard for weak mortals to
understand."

For a while they drank their tea in silence. In her
own heart Florence could not condemn Gregory.
Yet she knew he was in disgrace. In Victoria this
would be whispered about. Florence did not question the disgrace, but she accepted it without understanding. She thought that the squaw man from
Klawok must be a disreputable character, but she
knew that Gregory was not. Presently Ma began
to talk about Gregory, how he used to be when he
was a little boy, and they talked together about his
singing in the church choir in Victoria and about
the hopes they had had for him. They didn't say it
but each knew that the other was remembering how

Pa had never quite understood Greg. Pa thought that music was splendid as an accomplishment but that a man should develop in the more practical professions. Pa had always thought Greg a dreamer.

Florence's face was serious and her voice low. She felt a certain solemnity in this first conversation that was quite without any reservation made on account of her youth. In the mutual understanding of their women's hearts she and Ma knew that they would not give Gregory up, that they would wait. Florence told Ma that she would write to Beldon; she was sure Beldon would understand. She told Ma what Gregory had said, standing there on the stairs holding his candle. "Remember, when you tell Bel about this, tell him that I respect the Indians."

"He meant that—that—to his way of thinking, this is no disgrace," Ma said.

They both fell silent again, baffled and sad because it was so hard to understand. Then Ma sighed. "There is no need to grieve Pa with this until he gets back from his trip. That will be soon enough."

Florence nodded, understanding. Late as it was, they got up to go downstairs and begin the day again.

Alec and Jaimy came from the boathouse in response to Florence's call. Before there was time to speak, Jaimy looked from Florence to Ma. "What's happened?" he asked.

Alec gave them both a sharp look. "Now what
have you been crying about?" he asked. "Everything's been taken care of and in my opinion the
trouble was never as bad as Greg let on."

Ma sat down on the chair Florence had used
when she read Greg's letter. She put the store key
on the table and took Gregory's letter out of the
pocket in her skirt.

Suddenly Alec said very loudly, "Where's Gregory?"

The silence that followed his question was hard
and unbearable. Ma, looking weary beyond endu-
rance, seemed unable to reply.

"He went away this morning," Florence said
quickly, wanting to spare Ma.

But Ma rallied and with a quick intake of breath
she faced the boys and began. "Now, Alec, be
calm," she said. "I want you to read Gregory's letter, but first I want you to understand that Gregory's intention was honorable when he did this. I
want you to consider that before you remark on it."
She looked seriously at her oldest son. "Remember
that it is for God to judge, not for us." She handed
him the letter.

Jaimy stood beside him to read it. When Alec
finished, Jaimy took the letter and began reading it
again. Alec glared at him and at Florence as though
he were accusing them of complicity, but he didn't
look at Ma.

"He's daft, plumb daft!" he said, walking around

the kitchen in agitation. Suddenly he shouted, "He's made his bed, now let him lie in it. Why, he's no better than . . ." He pulled up in front of Ma. "I'll hold my tongue," he said, standing there awkwardly. "You ought to rest, Ma. Rest if you can." He turned abruptly and strode to the door. "He ought to be whipped," he muttered, almost hiding the break in his voice. A moment later they heard the hammer blows, hard and fierce as he worked in the boathouse.

Jaimy looked uncertainly from Ma to Florence and tears that he didn't seem to know were falling rolled out of his uncomprehending eyes. He put the letter on the table and with a supplicating gesture he said, "Look here, old Greg didn't mean to hurt anybody!" Then he knew he was crying and he dashed out of the door after Alec.

That morning a delegation of Indians came to request formally that they be allowed to bury Old Yelthnow's body on Our Point. They explained to Alec that Yelthnow had asked before he died that this be done because his spirit would then be with Mr. Monroe and there would be concord between them. Young Paul came with them and did most of the talking because Konutkan knew so little English. He told Alec that he had become a new man and offered him a twenty-dollar gold piece as a token of his reformation. "I go to Howkan and join church," he explained. "I good man now."

Alec looked at him sternly and declined the gold

piece. "You will have to prove that you are our friend," he said. "I will wait and see." But he saw no harm in their burying their respected old chief on Our Point. The Indians who had come from Howkan for that purpose prepared the grave and in the afternoon the funeral took place.

Ma's gray eyes were still full of pain and her face was sad but she marshalled her family. "We must go to the funeral," she said. "It is their gesture of peace. I feel—I don't know just why—that in these things of life and death we differ only outwardly."

Alec started to protest but there was something in Ma's demeanor that silenced him. They waited until the chanting, wailing procession had come around the beach from the Yelthnow house, until all the people, wrapped in blankets against the cold gray day, had gathered around the grave. Then, dressed in their Sunday clothes, the Monroe family took the trail that led around the new boathouse to Our Point. The grave was midway out on the point, and as they came near the Indians moved aside and the family stood near the grave with their heads bowed, as they would at a funeral at home.

It was a big grave, lined with cedar boards, and there were more boards stacked there to cover it. Yelthnow's most valued possessions, the things he had bought at Pa's store, were buried with him. He was sitting in the grave with a red blanket Pa had given him wrapped about him and a china lamp and a small factory-made trunk beside him. Ma gave a little gasp and clung to Alec's arm. The young men were erecting the Yelthnow family symbol, grunting and heaving as they planted the great carved wolf in the ground. It stood ten feet high, staring across the cove past the Monroe house to the village.

While the young men were erecting the totem, Ma began praying earnestly, as if to ward off its heathen spirit. "Our Father which art in heaven." Her quiet, steady voice formed the words with great distinctness. Jaimy and Florence prayed with her. "Hallowed be thy name. Thy kingdom come." Alec's deep voice joined them. "Thy will be done in earth, as it is in heaven." As they prayed, the wailing and chanting of the Indians ceased and they listened to the voices of the Monroes. When the prayer was ended, Ma walked to the widow of Old Yelthnow and touched her on the arm. "May God comfort you, and bring you the light of His love," she said. There was silence as she spoke. The dark eyes of the people of Klinkwan followed the Monroe family as they turned and walked back to the big white house.

Ma clung to Alec's arm, exhausted and pale, and Jaimy and Florence followed them. It was a long time since Florence had walked this way with her twin brother—like walking in the aisles of a church —and she felt strangely comforted.

The kitchen door was thrown open as they came to it and Einar Gren stood there holding it. The

fragrant smell of clam chowder greeted them as
they went in. "I took the liberty," he said bashfully to Ma, "of making a chowder to warm you."

Ma said, "How kind you are, Mr. Gren! It's just
the thing, just the thing to warm us up."

When the long day came finally to an end Florence sat up in bed with her cashmere shawl
wrapped around her and her writing case on her
knees. She had waited all day for this quiet moment when she could write to Beldon. She sat now,
leaning forward away from her pillows, writing
rapidly.

> Dear Beldon:
>   It's hard to tell you what I must tell in this letter.
> I need you—so terribly—to understand. I wish you
> had been here. It might never have happened if
> you had been here to talk to Gregory. Oh, I do
> need you to understand that I can never change
> about Gregory. Whenever I see him again—and I
> pray to God it will be soon—I shall be just the same
> to him.

Her pen flew as she wrote pages telling Beldon
about Jaimy's shooting the wolf and about the
trouble with the Indians. She tried her best to tell
him about Nakatla. She told him about her coming
to warn them and how Gregory felt he must protect
her. It was hard to tell him about Greg and Nakatla
because she couldn't really grasp it herself, Nakatla's ways were so different. Why, Nakatla was

heathen and she couldn't really imagine them together. She remembered the great smoky house
that had always been Nakatla's home and she
thought of the Monroe dining room with the old
silver and the china.

Oh, Beldon, it is all so difficult to understand. I
do wish you were here to talk to me about it. Gregory told me to tell you this when we talked last
night. I knew something was hurting him but I
couldn't tell what. He said, "When you tell Bel
about this, tell him that I respect the Indians." Ma
says that he acted honorably according to his lights
and I'm sure of it. I shall never give Greg up, even
if Pa disowns him. I miss him so dreadfully and I
know that Pa will never forgive him, never let him
come home again because he considers such an act
the worst possible disgrace. If only he would let
Gregory come home, we might be able to teach
Nakatla our ways. But that's dreaming. He never
will. It will break Pa's heart, but you know how
proud he is. He will never speak Gregory's name
again. But Gregory is my brother and if I see him
again I shall speak to him and if I can find where
he is I shall write to him. I have never disobeyed
Pa, but I will not give my brother up.

I know you will agree with me about this, but
I want you to tell me because my courage fails me
when I think of meeting Pa. The next boat will
bring him to Wrangell. If you get a letter on it, the
boys will bring it from Wrangell when they bring

him. Your letter will sustain me through this sor-
rowful time. My heart fails me when I think what
life would be without your love.

I am faithfully and ever yours,

Florence Monroe

CHAPTER *13*

*A*FTERWARDS, whenever Florence remembered the time that stretched between Gregory's going away and Pa's return to Klinkwan, she thought of the days measured off in yards of baby-blue outing flannel. Like the queens of old who worked away on their tapestries while battle and disaster approached their gates, she and Ma stitched on the blue flannel and waited for Pa, and for a letter from Beldon Craig. Gregory's name was not mentioned after the second day when Alec and Jaimy quarreled about him. The family kept silence like a shield between their hearts and their various ways of thought.

With the fire roaring in the big sitting-room stove
Florence and Ma talked about Laura and about
Florence's wedding as they basted the blue flannel
together. Florence had learned to sew a straight
seam now on the sewing machine. She liked the
whir as she pumped the treadle because it kept her
from thinking and eased her anxiety. Under their
industrious fingers the blue drawers and undershirts,
patterned after Pa's, began to pile up in finished
bundles, ready for the shelves of the store. But
often, as they worked, they would stop to gaze out
of the rain-streaked windows, each busy with her
own thoughts.

The boys waited for the weather to settle and left
for Wrangell to meet Pa on a day so calm that the
water lay like silver plate under the low, motionless
overcast. The cove was so smooth that the gulls,
flying low over the water, trailed reflections as
fragile as a breath on shining metal. In the still air
every little sound could be heard. The sibilant beat
of the ravens' wings was loud as the great birds flew
over the Monroe house. "That's a good omen," said
Ma. "The Indians say that when the ravens fly over
the house someone is coming. That means they'll
all get back safely."

Alec surveyed sky and sea with a canny eye. He
decided to go by way of Cape Chacon because, if
the calm held, they could make better time going
up Clarence Strait than they could weaving through
the islets on the outside.

"We'll get right out," he said, "and make it around Chacon before another blow comes up." He and Jaimy provisioned the *Laura M.*, loading her narrow decks high with wood. The skiff plied back and forth from the boat to the beach in front of the house, cutting the smooth water into dark swirls. They took load after load out to the little steamer to the delight and entertainment of the Indian children watching along the shore.

Ma urged Alec to take much more than enough food in case a storm came up and they had to run in somewhere and wait. She made shortbread and poundcake because they would keep well. During the preparations much of the grim patience that had settled upon the house vanished, because at last Pa was coming and everything would get straightened out one way or another. Ma gave Alec a letter for Pa.

"Tell him yourself if you want to, Alec," she said, "but give him this letter." It was a thick letter and Alec put it in his pocket. Nothing more was said until they were leaving.

As he was bidding them good-by Alec looked sternly at his sister. "You'd better fatten up, Flossie," he said. "Pa will not be pleased to see you looking so washed-out." To Ma he said, "Mr. Gren will stay here in the house and every day or two he'll open the store for an hour. That'll give the Indians time to buy what they need. There's lots of wood in the shed. Take care of yourselves well and don't worry. If we're late getting back it will be for some good reason."

Florence walked down the beach to the skiff with Jaimy while Alec stood talking to Ma. "Oh, Jaimy," she said, "if you should see him—if you see Greg, tell him we miss him. Find out about him, Jaimy." She spoke in a low voice, trying not to sound too anxious.

"I'm going to look for him," Jaimy said. "I'll look for him everywhere. If I find him we'll figure out some way to keep in touch without Pa knowing."

Einar was waiting in the skiff and Alec came then and they could say no more. But Florence was exhilarated and almost happy. She stood looking at Jaimy's face and she realized that Jaimy did not consider Gregory a disgrace. But Jaimy was too young to realize—here she stopped, astonished. Why, Jaimy was her twin brother; he too would be eighteen in June. Oh, but Jaimy had never been in love, Jaimy had never suffered, she thought, looking at him as he stood there waving good-by again to Ma and smiling. Then he made a little gesture to Ma, who stood on the porch watching them. He winked at her and with his closed fist he pushed his chin up as far as it would go. Ma laughed and called to him, "Come back as fast as you can."

Florence walked up to the porch and stood on the steps below Ma, watching as Einar Gren rowed her brothers out to the *Laura M.* They had had steam up for an hour and smoke was pouring out of the tall, thin stack. With the dinghy lashed to the cabin and wood stacked all around the deck, the *Laura M.* was like a little fat lady carrying innumerable baskets on her way to market. As she steamed out of the cove Alec pulled the whistle cord. She gave out a puff of steam and a deep, confident rumble. Einar rowed back to the beach and the *Laura M.* proceeded out through the Narrows. She turned and disappeared around the end of the island, leaving a white, foaming wake on the still water.

"I believe Jaimy will find Greg," Ma said. "I believe he will." She went indoors, cautioning Florence not to stay out in the cold.

Florence followed Ma into the house. "He *is* going to look for Gregory," she said. "But Ma, how did you know?"

"It was a bad hurt to Jaimy to lose his brother," Ma said. "Jaimy will never give him up."

After a week they began to watch for the *Laura M.*, looking out through the Narrows. They would go separately to the windows and watch the gray rain fall, each trying to hide her concern from the other. The *Laura M.* might not be back today, but surely she would be here soon. They were almost at the end of the yards of blue flannel and Ma had stopped sewing in order to do the baking against the return of Pa and the boys. They had grown tense and would fall into long silences. Florence knew that Ma was worrying about Pa. She too thought of him, but most of all she was waiting for Beldon's letter, for the reassurance it would give her.

One morning she went into Ma's room and found her standing at the window holding back the lace curtains and gazing out. Hearing Florence's footsteps, she turned and there was such longing and sadness in her gray eyes that Florence was overwhelmed again by their loss. She ran and threw her arms around Ma and they stood together looking out at the wintry islands. The wind had changed and the gray clouds moved slowly toward the southwest. As they watched, comforted by their mutual sympathy, the snow began to fall, the first snow of the season.

It fell in a flurry of big flakes, drifting over the hill back of the house and outward over the old houses of the Indian village. The white snowflakes, falling in a scatter out of the sky into the still, glassy water of the cove, vanished without leaving a trace on the smooth surface. Then, soundlessly, the wind struck the water a million invisible blows until its surface shone like hammered silver. The snow flew out across the point in light, fluttering flakes, through the totem poles and over the water beyond, growing thicker and thicker until it veiled the dark islands and the burial point.

"The snow!" said Ma with delight. "Look, the snow!"

They drew the curtains farther back and, arm in

arm, stood watching the snow sweep lightly out across the islands, watching it whiten one side of each sloping roof in the Indian village and cling lightly to the cedars on Our Point. The blue smoke from the roof vents of the old houses rose and drifted seaward through the delicate commotion of tumbling, spinning snowflakes. Soon the distant islands were lost to sight and the snow fell thickly into the cove, piling up comically on the carved beaks and heads of raven, bear, and wolf. The totem poles lost their singular sinister aspect and took on a humor that was almost gay. A sweet quietude stole over the village and crept into the hearts of the two women standing at the window.

"My, it's peaceful," said Ma.

All day the air was full of the minute white flutter of snowflakes. They came from the northeast on a wind born in the high, cold ranges of the mainland. All day they fluttered out over the islands. They clung lightly to the dark needles of the hemlock and the spruce and lay gently on the drooping boughs of the cedar. The air was filled with swirling, airily tumbling snowflakes that settled on the bent yellow grass above the tide line, turning it into a white ruffle around the dark shale. The snow piled up deeper and deeper on the roof of the Monroe house and whispered against its windows, drifting up at an angle along the kitchen sills and standing in white puffs on each garden fence post. Through it the gulls flew like ghosts, trailing their cries, but the black ravens took to the forest for shelter.

Along the walk between the boathouse and the door, Einar Gren's big footsteps soon filled up until they were only long white dents marking the path. The walk to the store was white and straight, with no mark upon it except where a scatter of late red berries from Pa's rowan tree lay in the little pockets where they had fallen. Protected under the spruce, the autumn-red salmonberry leaves still clung in a mass of color to their tawny stems, with snowflakes hanging like bits of fluff to the edges of their outermost leaves. At the end of the walk the store building stood bright and substantial in its red paint, with the snow drifting close around its idle chimney. In the Monroe house Einar Gren kept the wood boxes full and fires crackled in all the stoves.

During the night the wind increased, driving the snow against the windows with a dry, sandy noise and moaning out over the islands to the dark sea beyond. In the morning Florence woke late to a stillness so intense that she lay listening. She lay deep in her blankets, feeling the air cold on her forehead, listening to the silence of the snow-covered world. Then she heard the distant rattle of the stove lids and she knew that Einar Gren had got up and was starting the fires. She heard Ma lighting her fire and then there was silence again and she knew that Ma had popped back into bed to wait until the room should warm. She jumped out of her snug blankets and, snatching up her clothes, fled across the hall to the comfort of Ma's room to dress.

Outside, the late winter sun shone across a world gleaming with snow and the islands lay like white ships on the shining water. The snow had drifted against the low houses of the village and covered the big canoes on the beach. Overhead the sky was deep blue and all the trees of the forest were sheathed in shining white. As the sun rose higher the land glistened in its light and the tall totem poles cast blue shadows across the snowy roofs of the houses. It was a wintry sun, reflected in delicate bands of pale gold on the crest of each running wave so that all over the bay its light was moving and changing. The air was clear and sweet and very cold.

When Florence got downstairs she found a pot of Einar Gren's strong coffee on the back of the range and the kettle singing comfortably. McDuff lay under the stove with his bushy tail over his nose. Outside, Donny barked, running in circles around Einar Gren as he shoveled snow off the walks. Ma came into the kitchen in her knitted hug-me-tight and she and Florence started preparing the breakfast. Everything seemed so peaceful, yet the air was charged with anxiety because they both knew that, with the storm over, they could expect the *Laura M.* by nightfall or by early morning at the latest.

"I'll be glad when Pa gets here and it's all over," Florence sighed.

Ma said nothing for a moment. When she spoke it was with deep concern. "You and Jaimy must be patient with Pa," she said. "It is difficult for the young to understand their elders. Pa will be terribly hurt in his pride and that's a hard hurt for a man to bear."

"It isn't as hard as losing my brother," Florence said. She spoke quickly, without thought. "I'm sorry, Ma," she added hastily, "but I can never give Gregory up."

"It is your duty to obey your father," Ma said. "Sometimes life demands sacrifices of us." She sighed. "Think well before you make a decision, lest you regret it all the rest of your life."

That afternoon while Ma was resting, Florence sat at the window watching for the *Laura M*. After the midday meal she had made thin mint wafers because Pa liked them, and the fragrance of mint extract lingered in the air. She had changed to her blue foulard dress and she was sitting on the edge of a chair, tensely watching. She had decided not to face up to Pa, but to wait until she had read Beldon's letter. She would be patient and try to keep her peace. Besides, Jaimy would know about Gregory and she could talk to him somewhere away from Pa. The sun had dropped behind the mountains of the big islands to the west and the short winter day was near its end when she saw the *Laura M.* come steaming into the Narrows.

She jumped to her feet and ran for the stairs. "Ma!" she called. "Ma, they're here!"

"I'm up, dear," Ma answered. "I see them."

Florence ran to Ma's room and stood breathlessly at the window as Ma donned her garnet silk.

"Get your warm coat, dear, and meet them on the beach," Ma said. "Oh, I'm glad they're here at last."

"Shall I go down alone?" Florence asked doubtfully.

"Of course, child," said Ma. "Hurry now, while I put out the tea things. We must have a cheerful house to welcome Pa."

CHAPTER 14

AS FLORENCE came out on the front porch, the red glow from the sunset fell softly on the snow around the cove. Clear rims of ice were forming along the edges of the steps where the snow had melted in the sun and there was a stillness over everything. The *Laura M.* came through the Narrows with the smoke pouring out of her tall, thin stack. She came slowly into the channel between the two points of the cove. Jaimy stood in the bow ready to heave the anchor. Einar Gren was rowing out to meet them. He rowed standing up facing the bow of the skiff and she could hear him shouting greetings. Suddenly she called, "Jaimy! Oh, Jaimy, have you got my letter?" But just then the anchor splashed overboard. Jaimy was busy with the lines and she could see that he had not heard her at all.

Hesitantly, she went down the snow-banked path to the beach, her hands clasped tightly together in her muff.

On the point some of the Indians had come out to watch the landing. The young men wore the wool jackets they had bought from the store but the old ones were wrapped in their blankets. They stood in little groups under the totem poles, watching silently. Staring back at them from the grave on Our Point was the great wolf of Yelthnow.

Florence went down to the water's edge and waited while the men loaded boxes and parcels into the skiff. Now, with Pa home, Greg's absence was painfully conspicuous again and she knew that they all would suffer the same loneliness they had felt at table the first few days he was gone. She longed to have Beldon's letter in her hands for comfort.

The skiff was coming in now with Einar at the oars and Jaimy standing in the bow ready to leap out with the line. Pa and Alec stood in the stern, looking shoreward. Florence waved her little muff and Jaimy yelled, "Hello, Sis!" Then, suddenly, the tears were blurring her eyes. I mustn't cry, she told herself angrily. I mustn't be a ninny and cry! She fought to control herself and, standing at the very edge of the receding tide, she waved again to Pa. "Welcome home, Pa!" she called tremulously. But he did not answer, and she remembered too late that he hated shouting back and forth from a distance. He stood in the stern, looking impatiently shoreward, and for a while only the click-clock of the oarlocks could be heard. Then the bow of the skiff crunched into the shale near her feet and Jaimy jumped out.

"I saw him!" he whispered.

Einar Gren got out and helped pull the skiff farther up on the beach. Thrilled with his news, Florence leaned close to Jaimy. "Did you bring my letter?" she asked, while Pa and Alec were climbing over the boxes to get out.

Jaimy looked at her blankly. "There wasn't any letter for you."

Never had Florence imagined such a possibility. Jaimy's words struck at her heart like an actual blow. Pa was out of the boat now and there was no chance of further talk with Jaimy, but she could not have spoken anyhow. For a moment she thought she would faint away. Pa stood facing her, taller than ever in his greatcoat and his high sealskin cap.

"Well, Flossie," he said, "ye've been well through it all and a comfort to your ma, I hope?"

"Yes, Pa," she answered, but she turned away from his penetrating gaze and stood with downcast eyes, feeling her heart thud painfully in her bosom.

He took her chin in his gloved hand and turned her face toward him. "Ye needn't mope," he said.

"Your brother has broken God's commandment and turned against his lawful father and reviled him. Ye'll waste no tears on the likes of him."

She tried to turn away again but he held her chin firmly and she stood in an agony of grief and helpless rage. Deserted by Beldon in this first test of their love, she was stunned and could find no words for defense of her brother.

"There'll be no threepin' or gloomin' about," Pa went on sternly. "Until such time as he repents his act and mends his ways he is no son of this house."

While he talked, Einar Gren, loaded with bundles, made off hastily, striding along the shoveled path to the back of the house. Alec and Jaimy stood where they were, looking down at their feet in silence.

Inexorably, Pa went on lecturing her as though he knew her sympathies were not with him. "If he had any shame in him, he'd no longer use the name he has disgraced." He let go of her chin and looked around at the three of them. "We'll have no talk about this and no carrying on to distress your ma. There's not one of ye worth the end of her little finger." Again he addressed himself to Florence. "It does not please me, Flossie, to see ye standing there looking peaked and wispy like a deserted bride."

Like a deserted bride! She wanted to shout at him, "I *am* a deserted bride! Do you think Beldon wants to marry me now?" But she felt herself gasp-

ing for air and she sank down on the gunwale of the
skiff. All she wanted was for Pa to go away and
leave her alone. "I'm all right, Pa," she said.

"Nonsense, child," he replied, his voice softening.
"I can see you're pale and moony. Come, dry your
eyes. I've brought your pretties from the best shop
in San Francisco. Have no fear. Ye'll have a fine
wedding." He turned and went up the beach and
along the snow-banked path to the porch.

Speechless, Florence stared after him. Her pretties! A fine wedding! Could it be possible Pa would
try to force Beldon to hold to his promise?

The door of the house was thrown wide open and
there stood Ma in her garnet silk. "Welcome home,
Ian," she cried, holding out both hands to her husband. She had lit the lamps, and all the windows
were glowing in the half-light of the evening. She
had even lit the hanging lamp in the hall. As he
reached the door, Pa's tall silhouette hid her from
view. They had each other for comfort and understanding.

Florence got up and stood beside Jaimy, too mis-
erable for tears. "Are you sure there was no letter
for me, Jaimy?" she asked.

Jaimy shook his head. "I went to the post office
myself," he told her.

The sunset glow was gone now and all around
them the snow lay blue-shadowed and cold. Alec
hoisted a heavy box on his shoulder and started off.
"Brace up, Flossie," he said. "You both should re-

member that Pa expresses himself strongly when he's overwrought." He walked away, leaving them silent on the beach.

Jaimy began to rummage around in the skiff, gathering up the remaining bundles. "Greg's all right, Sis," he began. "That is, at least he's well. I didn't get to talk to him alone."

"Oh, Jaimy, I wish you had. I did want him to know that we'll never desert him!" She felt a closeness to Gregory now that she had not felt before— the closeness of exile and loneliness.

"I'll tell you how it was," Jaimy said. "First of all we met Pa. He'd got there a day before we did and we found him at the preacher's house. I looked for Greg but he wasn't in Wrangell. They told me at the post office that he had the job of running the mail boat that goes around Loring way. They said he wouldn't be back until next day." Jaimy stamped his cold feet on the beach and leaned one knee on the skiff's gunwale.

"What did Pa say when you told him?" Florence asked.

"Alec told him," Jaimy said. "He told him everything, about the Indians and all, you know—as he sees it. Pa sat there on a stiff chair in the preacher's sitting room listening. Alec kept on talking even about Old Yelthnow's funeral and everything— everything except that Greg had gone." He paused and pulled his cap farther down over his ears. "Pa hadn't said a word," he went on. "Then suddenly he leaned forward and plunked a hand down on each knee, keeping his eagle eyes on poor old Alec. 'Come, mon,' he says, 'oot wi' it! What are ye holdin' back?' "

Jaimy imitated Pa so exactly that Florence laughed in spite of herself, but she was sorry for Alec, too. She waited for Jaimy to go on, not wanting to go back to the house and begin thinking again.

"Well, Alec told him, and he told him how broken up Ma was that day when she found Gregory's letter. I must say that Alec tried to be good about old Greg, but all the same it sounded pretty bad, as if Greg'd done something we could never live down."

"What did Pa do?" Florence asked in a whisper.

Jaimy paused, his young face troubled and grave. "He—he looked as if Alec had hit him," he said. "He ducked his head, just as if Alec had taken a swing at him." Jaimy sighed and began to gather up the parcels. "We sat there like bumps on a log," he went on, without looking at her. "Then Pa jumped to his feet and yelled, 'What are ye doing sitting there? Get down and load the boat!' Alec gave him Ma's letter and we went out, leaving him standing there looking at it." Jaimy looked up at her. "Pa's awful pig-headed, Sis," he said, "but I felt sorry for him when we left him alone. I'd never seen him look like that before."

"But Jaimy, you said you saw Gregory. Where

did you see him?" Florence hugged her little muff close to her for warmth.

"I did see him. I saw him the next day when Pa and I went to the post office," Jaimy said. "We were just coming up the walk to the door when who should we meet coming out but old Greg himself. I forgot he's supposed to be so bad and I grabbed him by the hand. He asked about Ma and I said she was all right. Then Pa pulled me away and shoved me right off the walk! I thought a bear had hit me."

"What did Greg say? How did he look?"

"He didn't have *time* to look," Jaimy snorted. "Pa started right in on him, quoting the Scriptures the way he does, and telling Greg how sinful he was to hurt Ma and disgrace the family. Then he said it was not for him but for the Almighty to judge the unrepentant sinner. Greg took that all right but he was cold as a stone before Pa had his say out."

Florence waited for him to go on, feeling the cold creeping through her boots. Her feet were aching with cold but she hadn't noticed it until now.

"Pa told Greg if he'd mend his heathen ways and repent he could come home again. He meant it as a concession, I suppose, but it made Greg furious.

"Greg looked Pa in the eye and he said, 'My only regret is hurting Ma. I've done no wrong in the eyes of God—only in the eyes of hypocrites,' and he marched off down the street. Pa opened his mouth but he didn't say a word. He hasn't mentioned Greg's name since."

Jaimy started walking up the beach and then stopped to look back at her. "Don't look like that, Sis," he said. "I don't think Greg's done anything so horrible."

"Oh Jaimy, everybody else thinks so, everybody!" She started slowly after him, dreading to go into the house.

"What do you mean, everybody? I don't and you don't and I bet Bel won't."

"That's just it—I wrote to Beldon and told him that I could never give Gregory up, no matter what he did. He didn't answer, Jaimy. I begged him to send his answer on this boat, but he didn't. I never believed—I never thought that Beldon might not care for the sister of a . . ."

"I don't believe it!" Jaimy said crossly. "Bel's no fool. Why, I left a letter for Greg at Wrangell. I told him we were standing by him, Bel too!" When Jaimy was baffled he grew angry, and now he threw open the door and marched in ahead of her, muttering, "I don't believe it!"

With a quick glance at the sitting room, Florence went on up the stairs. Pa and Ma were sitting in there, talking and drinking their tea. They'll go on as though nothing had happened, Florence thought. Pa will do as he always has done—just not mention the things that hurt his pride. He'll go about just as though nothing had happened. She threw herself down on her bed, forlorn beyond crying. She knew that she must rally. She must think of a way to make Pa release Beldon from a promise that had become odious to him. But all she could feel was the pain in her heart and she lay on her bed in the dark until Ma called to her to come down and help with the supper.

At supper Pa talked about Victoria, about seeing Laura there and how improved he thought she was. He told them that the captain of the boat would bring Laura home on the spring trip. He told them about San Francisco, and after supper he looked at Florence. "You're over pale, Flossie," he said, opening one of the packages he'd brought. "Here's something I bought from a mon on Market Street. A woman is o'er frail and needs a tonic to put iron in her blood."

He insisted on dosing both Ma and Florence with a spoonful of the bitter stuff then and there and at every meal thereafter. Florence submitted but she knew it would not help her. Nothing would help her until she found the courage to give Beldon his freedom with dignity and understanding.

After supper she was glad when Pa began reading aloud out of the Bible. There would be no time to talk and soon she could retire to her room and try again to think it all out. Pa chose the fifteenth chapter of the Gospel according to St. Luke. Florence knew that he had not chosen it by accident. When he began reading the part about the prodigal

son she knew that he meant to convey to them all
that if Gregory would repent and return home he
would take him in again. But how could Gregory
repent if he did not feel that he had sinned? She
glanced at Ma, who sat in her rocking chair, darning the boys' socks. Ma's expression was quiet and
resigned. It was hard to tell if she was listening or
if she was occupied with her own grief. She would
write to Beldon and tell him that she had not
thought about the disgrace when she wrote before.
She waited impatiently for Pa to finish, so that she
could go to her own room.

But when she got to her room she found that she
was weary beyond expression and she could not
find the words to say what was breaking her heart.
She lay in the cold, dark room trying to sleep, wanting more than anything to sleep and in the magic of
sleep to find that nothing had changed, that everything was as it had been before Gregory went away.
But she could not sleep. Her mind was haunted by
the sudden dreadful realization that Beldon found
Gregory's behavior unacceptable. This thought had
never occurred to her until he failed to answer her
letter. Now she was grief-stricken that it could be
so and humiliated because she had not thought of
it when she wrote to Beldon. She thought of his
sister, of a small picture he'd shown her of his sister
mounted on a horse, with her long riding skirt flowing down from her knees. She thought of Beldon's
aristocratic mother, whom she had never met. And

she thought of Gregory. She wanted to protect him —Gregory with his dark, curly hair, with his gray eyes defying the whole world. She would write to Beldon releasing him from his promise. She would tell him that she did not expect him to share their disgrace, that she loved him enough to let him go. But she could not cast aside her brother. She must see him when she could and she would not exclude his wife.

This was further than Florence had thought at any time before about her feeling for her brother Gregory. Alone in the cold darkness of her room she faced it out. I am the sister of a squaw man, she whispered. She lay staring into the dark with eyes wide open, trying to face her ruined life. She felt no shame; even when she said it she felt no shame. But she was bewildered and desolate that her life could be broken in this way. She knew she could not go on living as she had. She must go away. She would become a missionary nurse and dedicate her life to the heathen people of the world, even if she had to defy Pa to do it.

Defy Pa! Finally, now that Gregory was driven out, now that she had lost Beldon, she would defy Pa. Her throat contracted suddenly and painfully. For a moment she didn't realize that the dry sobs she heard were her own. Her heart was breaking and she lay in an agony of grief and pain for which there was no comfort. She lay face down, clutching her pillow, trying to stifle her sobs. But her strength gave way and she collapsed into uncontrollable weeping. Beaten by the violence of her grief, she could struggle no longer. Gasping convulsively, she turned her face from the soaked pillow and lay wildly sobbing. Tears, flooding from her eyes, ran across her temples and down her cheeks, drenching her mouth with the bitter salt of her despair. Her future lay in ruins from which the only salvage could be a life of self-sacrifice.

CHAPTER   *15*

WITH the fire roaring in the big sitting-room
stove, Florence drew the desk away from the wall
and turned it at right angles to the side window.
From this window she could see the store, with the
snow on its roof and the wood smoke pouring out
of its chimney. Pa and Konutkan were there and
Florence knew that if ever Pa missed Gregory it
would be at times like this. There was no one to act
as interpreter now, with both Greg and Nakatla
gone, and Young Paul at Howkan where he was
staying for the winter. But Pa would pretend that
it had never been any different and he would struggle with the few words of common language he and

Konutkan had, because Pa had such a power of
pride. She didn't want Pa to see her writing this
letter to Beldon; she didn't want anyone to see her,
because this was the saddest moment of her life.
She was writing to tell Beldon that she was going to
give her life to God's work in the missions in foreign
lands. She must make him understand that she did
not expect him to share the disgrace of the Monroe
family but that she would love him always.

"Dear Beldon," she wrote and then she sat with
the pen lying idle in her hand as she gazed out of
the window at the store. She was thinking of Gregory and of how difficult it was to say what·she
wanted to say. She felt profoundly sad, but in her
heart she knew that she was not ashamed of Gregory. She was puzzled, recognizing the disgrace but
not understanding her feelings about it. The disgrace was there but it was in another category—beyond Greg's control, like an earthquake or a tidal
wave, apart and separate from him. She tried to tell
Beldon how she felt and that she knew the world
would judge Gregory otherwise. She even tried to
tell him that Nakatla was beautiful and that she
could learn to be a Christian. But the words of her
letter were stumbling and confused because she was
trying to say more than she knew how to say. When
she finished it she was in tears.

Still Florence dared not tell Pa of her decision.
He was less grim after his talk with Konutkan and
he was mightily pleased with the work Einar Gren

and the boys had done in his absence. He praised Ma and Florence for their work on the blue flannel and he carried the blue undergarments to the store himself. Florence kept waiting, hoping that a time would come when it would not be so difficult to talk to Pa. He behaved now as though Gregory had never existed and she did not know how to begin talking to him. Besides, she was afraid of his wrath. She went through the ordeal of taking the hated tonic after each meal, but day by day she grew paler and more wistful.

Pa had been home for more than a week when Ma came upstairs one morning to find Florence standing at the window gazing sadly southward. It had become her habit of late to slip away when the work downstairs was done and stand at her window looking out across the bay, listless and dreaming. On this morning the wind had changed and the cold spell was broken. Great puffs of cloud blew in from the south, sailing swiftly over Klinkwan with the sunlight flickering through their passing shadows. All morning the warm wind had increased until the long clear icicle hanging from the eaves above the window began to melt and drip slow crystal drops from its dagger-like point. The rustle of silk in the doorway made Florence turn. She saw Ma looking at her with grave concern.

"Florence dear," Ma said, "I am worried about you. You will go into a decline if you continue to grieve like this. Come into my room. We'll try on

your new gowns and talk. Unburden yourself, child.
You and I must support each other."

They carried the gowns, the cloaks, the bonnets,
and the dainty undergarments into Ma's room. Pa
had been lavish in his purchases; it was a trousseau
fit for a princess.

"The things are a little frivolous, I'm afraid," Ma
said. "I suppose it's because Pa bought them in San
Francisco. I didn't think to advise him to buy your
trousseau in Victoria."

Florence held up her arms as Ma pulled a flowered challis morning dress down over her head.
"You're thin, dear," Ma said, tying the blue satin
sash so that the long end fell on either side of the
bustle.

On the bed lay the white wedding dress with its
tulle veil and the little half-wreath of wax orange
blossoms. Florence looked at herself in the looking
glass and began to cry. She could contain herself
no longer. She poured out the whole story: her letter to Beldon; her determination not to abandon
Gregory; her unwillingness to go on with the wedding plans now that she was the sister of a—she
couldn't say the word. She told Ma of her desire to
give her life to good works and how she had been
afraid to tell Pa because she thought he would insist
upon the marriage and that Beldon would be too
gallant to refuse.

As she talked, Ma sought a chair and sat down.
When she finished, Ma said, "Have you been griev-

ing all this while because you think Beldon's love has failed you?"

"Oh Ma, at first I didn't! But when no answer came to my letter begging him to support me, then —then I was afraid."

"I hadn't thought," Ma said slowly, "that Beldon would change. Are you sure, dear, that there was time for him to answer your letter?"

"There's been another mail," Florence said, "and there was no letter. Oh Ma, if he would only write —if he would just write *anything!*" She turned again to the window.

"You must have faith," Ma said. "Beldon must have some reason."

Suspended between hope and despair, between desire and renunciation, Florence gazed out of the window, bewildered that her life should have come to this. She longed to go away—to keep on going forever and ever, to sail away to the Mediterranean, to Spain, to Suez, to all the exciting places she had ever heard of and never to stop. She looked out over the gray, windy bay with the bars of sunlight flickering through the flying clouds. As she watched, the outermost of the Barrier Islands seemed to detach itself from the group and move toward Klinkwan. For a while she stared at it, not realizing that this was not an island—it was a ship.

She reached to the table by the window for Pa's binoculars. She held them to her eyes and a rush of gray and white swept across the lenses. Nervously

she tried to focus them and finally she saw the
islands, snow-covered, with a band of black rock
between them and the sea. She followed the long
stretch of islands out to the last one and then,
framed in the black circle of the glasses, she saw
the ship, a black ship, schooner-rigged, sailing before the wind.

"Captain Craig's schooner," she said aloud. She
spoke as if to herself, and as she watched the perfect picture in the small rim of the glasses she felt
an inexpressible joy. "He's coming!" she whispered.
"Oh, Ma, he's coming!"

Ma came and stood by her side, looking across
the bay. "What is it, Florence? What is it, child?"
she asked anxiously.

"Look, Ma! Look out there between us and the
farthest island. There, in the south. It's the Craigs'
schooner—the *Lady Grace*!"

She took the binoculars down from her eyes and
the schooner receded and became a moving white
spot on the gray water. She handed the glasses to
Ma.

"I can't use those things, dear. I never am able
to see through them." Ma continued to peer out
over the bay and then her eyes concentrated on a
spot. "I see it now," she cried. "It's a sailing ship
of some sort. Call Jaimy. Jaimy's very good at telling the different ships."

She herself ran across the hall to Florence's room
and threw open the window on the side that faced

the boathouse. "Jaimy!" she called. "Yoo-hoo! Oh, Jaimy!"

Florence didn't move. She couldn't have torn herself away from the window if she had tried. She raised the glasses and stood watching the schooner until her arms grew tired. It *was* the *Lady Grace*! She didn't need Jaimy to tell her that. She was trembling with excitement as she watched. Did he come in sympathy or in anger? Oh, it was better for him to come in anger than not at all.

She heard Ma's voice. "Come here, Jaimy. There's a ship coming. We want you to see if you can recognize it."

In a moment Florence heard Jaimy coming up the stairs. She stood silent and shaken, while Ma hastily gathered up an armload of undergarments and threw a cloak over them.

Jaimy bounded in. "What's all the excitement?" he asked. "What the deuce is going on anyway?" He looked around at the confusion of gowns and tissue paper.

Florence handed the binoculars to him. "Look, Jaimy—coming in from the south. It's Captain Craig's schooner."

He took the glasses and looked through them to the south. "It's a schooner, all right," he said. "Man, she's coming at a pretty clip! Set straight for here, too. Must be the Craigs! Anyone else but Bel would pull in to Hunter Bay with a ship that size." He thrust the glasses into Florence's hands. "Take a good look, Sis." He grinned. "He must have got your letter."

He dashed out of the room, going down the steps two at a time with great thumps. "I'll tell Pa and Alec," he called back.

"You—you didn't *ask* Beldon to come immediately, did you, dear?" Ma asked.

"Oh no, Ma. I asked him to write and tell me that he understood that I couldn't desert Gregory —no matter what. He hasn't had time to get the second letter. I wish I knew—I wish I knew how he feels about it all." Florence continued to watch the schooner, wondering how ever she could stand the suspense of waiting until Beldon should come ashore.

Both of the boys came upstairs with Pa to look out over the islands to the bay beyond. Pa took up the binoculars and wiped the lenses with his pocket handkerchief. Then he looked long at the ship. "What could be bringing Captain Craig north again so soon?" he mused. He handed the glasses to Alec and turned to regard Florence with an inquiring eye. "Flossie, no doubt ye've written to Beldon concerning the events of the winter," he said. "Did ye say aught that would bring him rushing back from his visit wi' his family?"

The three Monroe men seemed to fill Ma's room, and Florence felt the color rush to her face as they all turned to look at her. "No, Pa," she said. "I asked him to write, that was all."

"So that was all, was it? Ye said nothing and he comes racing up north with his father's schooner in the middle of winter! Come, Flossie, ye might as well confess it if ye've been crying to the Craigs that ye've been misused."

"Oh, Pa, I didn't!" She tried to face Pa's eyes but they seemed to bore right through her and make her feel ashamed, although she knew she had nothing to feel ashamed for. "I just wanted him to understand—I wanted him to know . . ." She was stuttering like a frightened child and she was angry and humiliated.

Suddenly everyone was embarrassed. Jaimy and Alec left the room awkwardly and went downstairs. Pa glared at Florence. "I'll have this out wi' Beldon Craig when he arrives," he said. "And mind ye, Flossie, ye'll learn to behave like a proper Monroe before ye leave this house to be wife to any mon!" He stalked out of the room.

Florence stood staring at the door through which he'd gone, no longer able to ignore the resentment that seethed within her. "I'll talk to Beldon," she said, "and I'll talk to him alone." Impulsively she turned to Ma. "Pa has no right to boss us around so," she cried. "I can't face Beldon before the whole family—just as though nothing had happened. I won't let Pa make it seem as though Gregory had never been born."

"Try to be patient with Pa, dear. It is hard for

him to understand the young." Ma looked at her beseechingly. "Don't look so fierce, dear. Pa was angry because you acted without advice. He forgets what it is to be young."

Florence looked again at the schooner flying in toward Klinkwan. In broken masses the clouds raced across the bay above it and the changing bars of sunlight shone through them, sometimes on the white sails of the ship and sometimes away from it, brightening the foaming water of the bay. In the warm wind the snow was melting and running in trickling streams across the dark beach. "I don't know what I'll do if Pa lectures me before Beldon," she said, staring miserably at the deserted beach. "I couldn't bear it. I've got to talk to Beldon alone."

Across the cove the Indians began to come out of their houses. All of them were dressed in baby-blue outing flannel. The women wore the undershirts and the men wore the trousers. The tails of the shirts and the ends of the long legs and sleeves had been cut off and made into small garments for the children. Ma came over to comfort her daughter and she caught sight of the population on the beach.

"Good gracious!" she exclaimed. "They're wearing the nether garments on the outside. Mercy! Look at them. The babies and all!" For a moment they both stared. Then Ma burst into laughter. "Oh, dear," she laughed, "oh, dear me!"

But Florence did not laugh. It seemed to her that

her position was becoming more ridiculous every
minute. If the Indians had dressed up to greet the
ship they would all be on the beach when Beldon
came ashore. She would have to greet him not only
with the family watching her but with the whole
population of Klinkwan, too—in those absurd blue
drawers. "Oh, Ma, how can you laugh?" she cried.
"There's not even a shred of dignity left to me. Oh,
I can't face it."

With an effort Ma controlled herself. "Come,
dear," she said, putting her arm around Florence's
waist, "there's no use being so upset before anything has happened. Put a pinny over your new
gown and come and help me get the dinner. It'll
all work out."

The *Lady Grace* was almost an hour out, and
while Florence was helping Ma prepare the noon-
day meal she made trip after trip upstairs to look
out of the window and see how close the schooner
had come. She was in an agony of suspense, full of
hope and full of dread lest Pa humiliate her before
Beldon and his father. She was ashamed of herself
for failing to speak outright to Pa. She wished she
had told him that she must talk to Beldon about
Gregory, because she had no intention of living as
though Gregory were dead.

Again she ran upstairs to the window and looked
out. The schooner was pulling in to the lee of the
outermost island beyond the Indian burial point and

Pa and Alec were rowing out of the cove in the big
skiff to meet her. The Indians were launching their
canoes to paddle out and look at the schooner.
There were moving patches of baby blue in the
cove and in the Narrows and all around the beach.
Florence yearned with all her soul to see Beldon,
but the prospect of meeting him there on the beach
filled her with a dread she could not control. They
would meet in all that confusion and come in and
have to sit through the dinner, and she knew she
would not dare even to look at him. She watched
Alec rowing Pa out around the Indian burial point
to the schooner lying at anchor.

Then she went slowly downstairs to tell Ma that
they would soon be in. Ma came and stood with
her on the porch. Jaimy and Einar Gren were on
the beach just below them. Presently they saw the
schooner's jolly boat come round the point into the
Narrows. They could see Pa and Captain Craig
standing in the stern and Alec and Beldon rowing.
Close behind came the skiff with four of the schooner's crew. Oh, it was cruel of Pa not to let Beldon
come in alone! It was cruel and it wasn't fair!

"Ma," she cried, "I can't meet him in front of all
those people. I can't!" In an agony of shyness and
sudden fright Florence brushed past Ma and ran
up the stairs to the sanctuary of her own room.

She shut the door and walked about the room,
her knees trembling and her heart going like a ham-

mer in her breast. Her sense of delicacy was mortally offended and her resentment against Pa's authority boiled within her. Everything seemed to her distorted and cruel, and this last indignity of Pa's was more than she could endure.

She caught sight of herself in the long looking glass of her dressing table, standing there in her finery, twisting her handkerchief into a tight little wad. She glared angrily at the reflection; then she threw the handkerchief down and began to struggle out of the dress. Oh, it was all right for Pa to be so self-righteous and to disown Gregory, to expect them all to fall in with his way of thinking. Here he was, bringing all those men ashore. To please himself he was making it work out so that she couldn't have a chance to see Beldon alone. He wanted her to greet Beldon in front of all those people as if nothing had happened. That's what he would call behaving like a true Monroe: to go down and meet Beldon as though nothing had happened —like strangers meeting.

She threw the new gown across the bed, took her old plaid skirt and blue bodice out of the wardrobe, and got into them. Then she looked cautiously out through the window curtains and saw that the jolly boat and the skiff were in the cove. She could not see Beldon's face but the sight of his lean shoulders brought the color to her own pale cheeks and strengthened her resolution. She pulled on her short

gum boots and got into her long woolen coat. Hatless, she ran down the stairs.

Ma turned and looked at her in astonishment.

"I'm going out, Ma!" she cried, not stopping. "Pa
can make any excuses he wants to. I'm going out."

CHAPTER 16

WITHOUT thought of the consequences, Florence ran through the dining room and out of the back door. She ran along the path to the boathouse and past it into the snow, hardly knowing what she was doing. She was making her first break for freedom and she was doing it in the only way she knew how. She had no time to consider that she was retreating in a panic. She knew only that she was seeking a spot where she could be alone, and where Beldon might find her. With the new building between her and the house she stopped in the snow to get her breath. She would give them time to land and go up to the porch and then she would make a

dash for the shelter of the cedars on Our Point. She
was exhilarated, and never before in her life had
she been so aware of her own identity. She, Florence Monroe, like a ship leaving port, was bound
outward now on the seas of her own life. Nothing
would be the same after this.

With a great intake of breath she started on
through the melting snow, slipping and sliding at
every step. She knew where the path led through
the cedars and she headed for it, leaving a trail of
wobbly footsteps behind her. She did not look back
toward the house. Holding her skirts in both hands,
she devoted her whole attention to reaching the
shelter of the trees. If they called her from the
house she would not turn.

But no one called. When she finally got under
the interlacing branches, the soft drooping branches
of the cedars, she was spent and gasping. She
stopped and, throwing her arms around the rough
trunk of a tree, she leaned against it, half laughing
and half crying.

Overhead the wind whispered in the cedars and
the lithe branches moved with a swaying liveliness
that had jarred loose the weight of snow, leaving
them free. The sound of the wind was soothing and
the air was sweet on Florence's face. In a little
while she had recovered herself. She found the
place where the trail went through the trees and she
sloshed along in the wet snow. She was shocked by
her lack of physical stamina, by her breathlessness

as she made her way to the far side of the point.
She had not been here since the bad weather set in,
and the bleakness of the place chilled her. Her ex-
hilaration began to ebb away. In summer the wild
crab apple and the salmonberry had brightened the
edge of the forest; the goosetongue and the wild
asparagus had made soft green patches on the dark
beach. But the leaves of summer had blown away
and only the somber evergreens stood above the
black rock of the shore line with their feet in the
melting snow. She walked along the beach to the
point where she could see out beyond the near
islands, out across the steel gray water to the wild
mountains of Hunter Bay. The sky was covered
with clouds now and a fine rain swept in across the
long chain of the Barrier Islands.

Nowhere was there a sign of human life. No
smoke rose to indicate a neighbor's house, and out
across the lonely bay no craft rode; only the sea
gulls soared in the rain-swept air above the sea.
Florence stopped walking and stood looking out
across the water.

Doubts began to assail her now that the excitement of her escape had died away. Suppose nothing happened. Suppose the afternoon should wear
on and Beldon fail to come. Suppose Pa had talked
to Captain Craig and Beldon and they had decided
merely to wait for her to come back. She would
have to return before dark. Wet and tired, she
would have to go back and face Pa, and everything

would be worse than it had been before. Oh, what could a girl do? What could a girl do for herself alone? It would be so humiliating, so undignified, to stay here and get soaking wet and then go trailing back.

Uncertain whether to go on or go back, she stood like a waif lost in the enormous indifference of the wilderness around her. Beldon and Pa and Gregory all pulled her heart in different directions and now she began to wonder if any of them really cared which way she went.

There was a rush of sound behind her and she turned with a start. Donny came racing along the beach, his curly ears flapping and his tongue out. He ran up to her, licked her hands, and immediately dashed back in the direction from which he had come. Florence turned and looked back toward Our Point. She saw Beldon Craig coming out of the drooping cedars onto the band of snow above the beach. He paused there and stood looking toward her with the white snow behind him. Without any warning, tears fell from her eyes and mingled with the rain on her face. Beldon started walking toward her and she toward him.

As they drew closer to each other she could see that he was not smiling; his face was grave and full of concern. Donny ran back and forth between the two, but they had eyes only for each other. Without words they met and Beldon took her hands in his and drew her to him. He took her in his arms and they stood in the rain clinging to each other and it seemed to Florence that her spirit had found haven at last. Beneath the comfort that Beldon's embrace brought to her, she felt a deep joy that this could be so, that it could be so without words. Anything they would say would be apart from this. The rain was on their lips when they kissed. It was her first kiss, tender and full of longing. When she drew away from him, they looked at each other, their eyes declaring their love. She saw that the mist stood on his fair hair in tiny droplets and that in the blue of his eyes there was tenderness and wonder.

He knelt down on the wet shale and took her hands and leaned his face against them. She sank down beside him, pressing her cheek against his hair. Brokenly she tried to tell him how she needed him, how when no letter came she had doubted his love, thinking that he, like Pa, had found Gregory's action intolerable.

"Oh, my darling," Beldon said, "I came the moment I read your letter. We sailed out that very afternoon, and we should have been here days ago but for the head winds. I couldn't write. I had to come. We'll find Gregory. When we have our own home we'll see him."

Kneeling there in the rain, they found the loyalties of their hearts and the truth in them, and they recognized each other's honor. Florence thought her heart would break for the faith she had not kept.

"I am not worthy of such love," she whispered.

"Oh, Beldon, I thought I knew what love is—but I have never known it until now!"

"Hush," he said, drawing her up to her feet. "Without you I couldn't even exist."

Arm in arm, they walked slowly back to Our Point. They talked seriously of many things, of their coming marriage and their future home, and of Gregory and Pa. Heedless of the rain, they paused often to stand enchanted in their mutual devotion.

Florence was full of wonder at this further discovery of love. She knew now that Beldon would fly to the ends of the earth to save her one moment's anguish. All that he did was faultless; all that he said was true.

As they came out from under the trees Beldon swept her up in his arms and carried her through the deep snow to the beach. He set her on her feet and they stood holding hands, breathless and laughing.

Across the cove the little children in baby-blue flannel gazed at them with solemn brown eyes. "Oh, they're sweet in the blue flannel!" Florence cried. She told Beldon about making the undergarments according to Pa's pattern—a pattern for a man six feet three inches tall—and how the Indian women had cut them off for the babies. Glowing and full of laughter, they approached the front of the house.

It was not until they reached the bottom of the

steps that Florence began to falter, feeling unprepared to meet Pa, feeling, somehow, not resentful
of Pa, but shy of him.

"Oh, Beldon," she whispered, "what shall we say
to Pa?"

She was holding his arm and he put his hand over
hers. He looked at her for so long without answering that she glanced away, blushing and recklessly
happy.

Finally he said: "I'm trying to think how I would
feel if I were your father. Suppose I were Mr.
Monroe, and some young fellow came along and
kept my beautiful daughter out in the rain for hours.
What would I do?" They both burst into laughter.
They arrived at the door laughing and were about
to open it when Pa opened it himself.

"Come in, young mon," he ordered. "Are ye going to keep my girl out in the rain all day? She'd
better come in and fix ye some victuals. Ye've
missed dinner."

"Yes, Pa," Florence said, sobering. She came into
the hall ahead of Beldon but Pa did not look at her.
For the first time she became aware that her clothes
were dripping and her hair was soaking wet—that
she must look ridiculous. But, for all she could tell
by his face, Pa was not aware of how she looked.

Beldon came in and closed the door behind him.
Florence could see smoke drifting in the sitting
room and hear the voices of men talking. Then
Captain Craig came out into the hall with his pipe

in his hand. His blue eyes were merry as he greeted
her. His dark whiskers were wild and bushy com-
pared to Pa's trim beard. Deep crinkles radiated
from the corners of his eyes when he smiled.

"Look at them, Mr. Monroe," he said, taking
Florence's hand, "walking in the rain and not knowing they're wet. It's a sight to remind an old man
of his own courting days." He chuckled and patted
the back of her hand.

But Pa did not look at them. He looked at Captain Craig. "Aye," he said, "a young woman needs
a guid mon to guide her—but a child still needs its
parents. We'll speak of the wedding in the evening
when the men have gone back to the ship."

"It's a dripping wet child should go and change
her clothes," Captain Craig said, giving her hand a
final pat.

Florence stole a glance at Pa, expecting to find
somewhere in his countenance a gleam of vexation
or disapproval—or forgiveness. But there was none.
He stood there, dignified as always and calm as ice.
He had not spoken one word to her directly. She
might have been invisible for all she could tell by
looking at him. He was trying to punish her with
silence. But she was free now and no longer angry.
She wished only that he would speak to her, that
he would stop being so stiff-necked and full of
pride. Pa was captive to his pride and he stood
there as if he could make his own stern attitude
settle over them all.

It was Beldon who broke the awkward pause. Taking Florence by the arm, he said, "Do you know who I am? I'm the guid mon who's going to guide you." Without more ado he steered her through the dining room toward the kitchen. "Mrs. Monroe," he called, "here come your errant children!"

That evening after the crew had gone back to the schooner and Einar Gren had retired to Beldon's sloop, the Monroe family and the two Craigs remained in the big sitting room. Florence and Beldon were on the little settee in the corner, where they had talked together in low tones while the conversation in the rest of the big room served as a shield for their privacy. But now it had grown quiet and they could not talk without being heard. There is a sense of victory in love and this sense was theirs. Even in silence there was a triumphant look about them as they sat enmeshed in their mood of happiness. Florence was in a sort of rosy dream and she was startled out of it by Pa's voice.

"Now, aboot this wedding," he said, and paused, looking at them all. "It is plain to see," he went on, "that my daughter Florence is a bit immature. It is plain to see she is not yet ready to take on the responsibilities of a married woman."

There was a dumfounded silence in the room following this observation of Pa's. Everyone looked at him as though expecting him to explain.

Jaimy turned suddenly and looked at his sister as though seeing her for the first time. "Why, Pa," he

said, astonished, "Flossie's grown up! Why, Flossie
kept house for us all at the saltery last summer and
the summer before!"

He hadn't quite finished when Pa cut in. "I'll
brook no interruption," he said, with a severe glance
in Jaimy's direction. "If ye canna listen, ye may be
excused."

Jaimy flushed and said no more. Ma stopped
rocking and looked at her husband. It was clear
that Pa was in a very bad frame of mind. He sat
straight in his chair and looked from one to the
other of them. "And furthermore," he continued,
"her ma is in frail health and needs her."

Florence looked at him in consternation. What
was he trying to say? How long did he mean her to
wait?

"Why, Ian," Ma said, "I'm in perfectly good
health. And I think Florence is just as capable, or
more so, to take up the duties of wifehood as I was
when I married you."

This was a very strong speech for Ma to make.
They all looked their surprise and Beldon smiled
outright. "Bravo, Mrs. Monroe," he cried.

"Nonsense!" shouted Pa, paying no heed to Beldon. "Nonsense, woman! Ye were raised in a time
when the young were far advanced to what they
are today."

Captain Craig had been sitting silent through
all this, but now he stood up, walked to the stove,
and stood for a moment warming his hands over its

shining black top. Then he turned to Pa. "With your permission, Mr. Monroe, I'd like to read from the Scriptures. When you said you would speak of the wedding tonight I mistook you. I thought the question of the marriage was decided. Certainly this afternoon your daughter's happy face did nothing to dispel my understanding. If there is aught I should hear, let me hear it. But first it is fitting to prepare ourselves with a verse or two from the Holy Book."

He held out his hand and after the briefest hesitation Pa handed him the Bible. "We have no lack of reading the Scriptures in this family, Captain," he said, "but it has little effect on the young for a' that."

Captain Craig took the Bible and drew a chair to the table. He put on his gold-rimmed spectacles and turned the pages with considerable certainty. Florence sat looking anxiously at Pa, wishing with all her heart that he would unbend and be gracious, for once. She felt Beldon's hand steal over hers and saw him wink ever so slightly. Then she turned away hastily lest Pa observe them.

The lamplight shone on Captain Craig's bald head and bushy face as he glanced over his spectacles at all of them before beginning. Satisfied that he had their attention, he began.

"The Epistle of St. Paul to the Ephesians, chapter six," he announced, and went right on reading in spite of a slight move from Pa's chair.

Children, obey your parents in the Lord:
    for this is right.
Honor thy father and mother;
    which is the first commandment with promise;
That it may be well with thee,
    and thou mayest live long on the earth.
And, ye fathers, provoke not your children to
    wrath:
    but bring them up in the nurture and
    admonition of the Lord.

"Amen," he said and closed the Bible. "I remember," he said reminiscently, "how sweet was life when I first knew my Mary. It's sorry I am she is not here to meet Mrs. Monroe and Florence."

"We shall meet some day," Ma said, without allowing time for a pause. "Oh, Ian! Remember what a time we had getting married? You were so angry with my father."

"Your father was a most unreasonable mon," said Pa. When no one spoke he went on, regarding Ma defensively. "Beldon Craig promised to wait for your daughter for a year. The year is not up until June."

"But Pa," Florence objected, "what can be gained by so long a wait?"

Pa looked at her sternly and she blushed, regretting her impulsive words. "Such haste is not becoming," said he. "I am glad to see you blush for your words."

Beldon jumped to his feet. Florence saw that he

was trembling with anger. "They are not Miss Monroe's words, sir," he said, "they are mine. It is true I promised to wait and I shall. But there is nothing indecorous in our impatience. Heaven knows it's natural."

Before Pa could reply Ma's voice broke in, gentle but persistent. "Ian," she said, "it is well to remember now that you and I eloped—and that my father never forgave us. Looking back, I am sorry that we were not more patient—and he more compassionate." She sat, small and quiet, looking at Pa with eyes full of memory.

"Ah, Maggie," Pa said, his voice filled with emotion, "if it will make ye happy, let them marry tomorrow. It was only for your good I was considering."

Florence looked at Pa, trying to imagine him young and dashing, carrying Ma off from her home in the Highlands against the wishes of a severe and angry parent. She had never thought of Pa in a romantic light before. "Oh, Pa!" she said. Then seeing him withdraw behind the curtain of his reserve again, she went on quickly. "Why, Pa, I have no wish to leave Ma before Laura comes home."

"Now, Flossie, that's the way I like to hear ye talk," he answered her, seizing upon this offer of compromise. He looked up at Beldon. "Young mon, ye need not be such a hothead. Our little Laura comes hame in April wi' Captain Hunter. By April

ye'll have time to fix a proper house at Thorne Bay
for my daughter."

"I shall wait, of course, sir," Beldon said, "with
the greatest impatience."

Ma began rocking again. "The Reverend and
Mrs. Douglas will be so pleased that the wedding's
to be in their little church," she told Captain Craig.
"Our children will be the first to be married in this
country in a proper Christian wedding."

"It is to be hoped," added Pa, "that the wedding
will have the desired effect upon the Indians and
that your lives," he looked toward Beldon and Florence, "will be an example of the true Christian marriage."

"Amen," said Captain Craig. "Now do you think
we might have a few songs before turning in? This
occasion must not be too solemn."

They had not sung together since Gregory went
away, but Florence got up now and went to the
organ. It would not be the same without Gregory's
voice. Everything was changing and she must begin to build a little bridge between the way it had
been and the way it would be on her wedding day,
a little bridge that would keep them all together
even though they left Pa's house.